Deep Condition

Elle Jeffries

ELLE JEFFRIES

DEDICATION

To my mother Tonya,
Thank you for carrying me then and now.

Deep Condition · Noun

1. The state of being black
2. An experience of the self that is shaped by pigment and history

^{2}Deep Condition · Verb

1. To engage in a preventative hair maintenance routine
2. To promote self-preservation

PROLOGUE.

Spring in the District felt like summer, tasted like freshly squeezed lemonade with agave, smelled like city. I stared out of the window of a coffee shop, sharing the view with a few strangers. My hands curled around a mug of tea, as I looked up at the clock. I guess I could wait a little longer.

Around the corner, Josephine scurried down the sidewalk with her notebook clutched under her arm. Her heel had gotten stuck in the sidewalk as she stepped out of her Uber – a frustrating addition to a morning full of unfortunate events. Flustered, she glanced at her watch and limped to the meeting with as much speed as her damaged shoe could handle.

She stopped and took a deep breath in the window of a bike shop. Her ebony skin glimmered in the sun as she straightened out a few of her misplaced curls. She smoothed out her lipstick and her dress before she stood with her back straight and walked into the coffee shop.

She spotted me before I saw her. Her heartbeat quickened, and she swallowed the lump in her throat as she approached the table we'd share. Josephine pushed her shoulders back and stuck out her hand. "I'm Josie."

I took off my glasses and looked up at her. She reminded me of me – a younger me, with large brown eyes that twinkled with wonder. She still had wonder.

"It's so great to finally meet you," she said.

I studied her before I smiled and nodded. "Yeah, you too."

Josie pulled out her notebook and pushed her hair out of her face. "First, let me apologize for all of my emails."

"Don't apologize. Your persistence paid off." She'd sent a dozen emails and managed to track down my phone number. Josie was a recent graduate of Georgetown, and new to the world of journalism. She was trying to get her online magazine off of the ground – a struggle that I knew very well.

She found a blank page in her notebook and positioned her pen to write. "Thank you for taking some time to speak with me. I've followed your work since I was in high school, from *Brown Girl* to *Pivot*. You're the reason I'm a writer. Now you've written a book and I hope that we can talk about it. But more than that, I want to know about you and how you got here," she said, while she slid her recorder between the two of us.

I smiled at the sight of the recorder, suddenly feeling nostalgic. I hadn't seen one in a while.

"It's been hard to pin you down for an interview," she said.

"Telling my story has never been easy."

The irony struck Josephine and she started the recorder. "Tell me more about that."

I'd made a career out of storytelling, writing and editing, erasing and rephrasing. I pulled and yanked at the edges of a narrative like I did my hair, twisting and curling until it felt finished. Until it fit into a shape I could wear, publish and sell.

With time I understood that there was beauty in every story, even when it was freshly washed and tangled.

When it wouldn't submit.

When it was *unruly*.

Josie leaned forward. She rested her elbows on the table we shared and smiled. "Where should we begin?"

Part I.
Eighteen.

Woman with a T.W.A.,
Woman with clipped stems,
Moisturize.
Flower.

CHAPTER 1.

"Remind me why you cut your hair off, again?"

I turned toward my mother as I hoisted a box out of the oversized move-in bin outside of my dorm. I shifted my weight to one side, and popped my hip out. A light mist had gathered on my collarbone and at the base of my neck. My mother's face had grown greasy during our seemingly endless treks between the car and the dorm. It was the middle of August and it was hot as hell.

"My hair was breaking off. We've talked about this," I said.

She ran her hand over my head with a touch more delicate than the first time she'd seen it. I'd cut the hair myself in front of the bathroom mirror with mascara-stained cheeks and trembling hands. I'd wanted to shed my skin in that moment, but I settled for the temporary comfort of trimmed strands instead.

"I think we could've saved it, Nia. I worked too hard to keep that hair healthy."

"It wasn't healthy," I mumbled, as I pushed the door of my dorm room open and stood in the middle of the floor.

I could smell the fresh coat of paint on the walls, and the worn wooden floors moaned as we settled in. The fluorescent lights caused my eyes to cross as I plopped the heavy box of clothes on the bed.

"How does it feel, Sweet Pea?" My mom sat down on the bare bed and allowed her lips to curl into a small, self-assured smile.

"To be here? I don't know."

I placed my hands on my hips and looked around at the mess I'd have to organize. The only life I'd ever known was shoved into boxes and bins, rolled up and wrinkled. I scoffed at the idea of making my *things* fit in this small room.

"You know…this reminds me of when I started school," she reminisced.

"Again?" I groaned. "You've told me this before."

My mother was a storyteller, too. Always had been. She'd twist my hair with coconut oil, her on the couch/bed/stool and me on the floor with a pillow beneath my knees. She would never let me sit directly on my knees – they were already too dark.

The pressure will make the dark worse, she'd say.

I'd listen to her words, to the sound of hair between her oiled fingers. The recollections rolled off of her tongue, soft and delicate. Her voice would dance into my pre-pubescent ears and I'd ask her things like…

"Why isn't our skin the same?" and…

"When will I see daddy again?" and…

"When did you fall in love for the first time?" I asked that more than once to hear how she would remember the story this time.

Her first love was a man named Johnson or Jonathan – the name escapes me now. They met in the summer. She teased her loosely curled hair to match the fros of her idols – Kathleen Cleaver, Angela Davis – and wore black despite the California climate. They met at a march or something like that – that changed every time she told the story. Johnson/Jonathan could quote Huey Newton and compliment her in the same breath. He was like a super Negro with arms the size of cannons.

My virgin shoulders hadn't been touched or caressed, but my gut grew tangled with anticipation when I listened to her. My intuitiveness for love and complicated shit started there on that floor in our sunroom. Johnson/Jonathan wasn't my daddy, but I often got the feeling that she wished he were.

She ultimately chose someone who looked like her father, and the two managed to birth a child almost in spite of who they were. My parents were butterscotch brown and I dangled in my dark with discomfort whenever I stood by them. Sometimes I'd catch my mother staring at her skin in the mirror, wondering if her pale countenance complicated her ability to raise me. But we were always close – she and I. In that sunroom, I grew to acknowledge the shape and size of a black woman's plight. I knew that my color couldn't be washed away, couldn't be scrubbed or lightened to butterscotch.

My mother was a storyteller.

She wove narratives and taught me life's lessons through parables about her own mistakes. She loved me before I loved myself and her love ran deep.

But it wasn't enough to stop the inevitable, for hearts and hymens would still break.

***

I stood on the front steps of the residence hall and watched as my mother climbed into the car she'd rented. Her flight to Madison was in a few hours, leaving me with an unfamiliar east coast breeze. I ran my hands over my arms, feeling goose bumps emerge. She idled in the car, studying me through teary eyes, before she rolled down the window and waved once more. I leant up against the railing and waved back with a limp hand. My eyes swelled with tears, but I turned to scurry inside before she saw me crack.

I wiped my eyes and walked swiftly through the hall to my room. My mother and I hadn't been apart longer than a few weeks at a time. We were the center of each other's universe. Despite our closeness, I distanced myself from her well before my cross-country move. A tragedy left me tangled and twisted with pain, and I hadn't shared any of it with her. I suffered in silence until it nearly strangled me. The suffocation led me to the bathroom sink with a pair of hair shears two nights before I was set to move to school.

That night, my hands removed the elastic band that held my long, straight strands in a neat ponytail. I tossed the elastic in the trashcan and took a deep breath. Even at the edge of an emotional catastrophe, I tried to keep my composure. Tears rolled down the sink while I made the first cut. The hair fell to the floor and I stood back and let out a sigh of relief. Slowly, I raised my hand and touched the rough ends of what I had left on my head. The tears froze on my cheeks and a small smile emerged.

As I walked back to my dorm room, the image of my mother's sorrowful wave stuck with me. I unlocked the door to find a girl with long, blonde hair there in the middle of the floor surrounded by boxes. She turned and glanced at me. "Hi," she said. She forced a smile and stammered a little – "I'm Olivia." She reminded of a girl I knew from back home, but the familiarity didn't bring comfort.

When I was born, my mother and father left California and moved to

Wisconsin. In kindergarten, I was the only black student in the class and the ratio didn't change much when I got to high school. In class photos, I was the black dot swimming in a sea of white. I was different and I knew that. My mother pushed me to feel pride but that wasn't easy.

In first grade I was attacked on the playground when a few white girls found out that a redheaded boy had a crush on me. In high school, I was berated with insults when I ran for class president. I lost by a long shot. I only got thirty-five votes – all from black students in our graduating class.

My mother was sure I'd attend a historically black college, but seemed relieved when I didn't get enough money to attend Howard. I'd gotten a full scholarship to attend Monroe – one of twenty-five students to receive the presidential diversity scholarship. With the scholarship, I was required to live in Mark Hall. Mark was known for its prized residents: children of cherished alumni, donors and the affluent.

Now, I stood in my dorm studying Olivia and wondering how she and I ended up here, together, in this small ass room.

I tossed her a head nod before I went and climbed onto my bed. "I'm Nia," I said. I pulled my feet close to me and folded my legs. "Where are you from?"

"Pennsylvania," she said, as she pulled her hair back into a ponytail and forced a smile – one of those tight-lipped, uncomfortable smiles. She looked at the door nervously. I pulled apart the discomfort that seemed to manifest in the rosiness of Olivia's cheeks as the door to the room opened, revealing her parents. Both of their faces flushed crimson when they saw me sitting there. Like their daughter, the two stumbled with surprise. "Oh, hello roommate!"

I tried to smile but my face remained flat. "Hello," I said, waving a little. The three of them exchanged glances.

"I'll let you get settled in," I said to her. "If you want to grab dinner, Olivia, we can walk over to the dining hall next door when you're all moved in." I hopped off of the bed and slid into my flip-flops.

"We've already made dinner plans. A reservation, I mean," she said, before she pointed to her parents.

I nodded. "That's cool. Enjoy." I smiled a little and left the room. I shut the door behind me and sighed, looking up and down the hall as it buzzed with freshmen moving into their rooms for the first time.

I tightened my grip on my wristlet and strolled casually down the hall, peaking into the rooms, looking for someone who resembled me. I went outside and resumed my spot on the front steps where I'd watched my mother leave moments earlier. My long, mahogany legs swung as I draped them over the concrete railing. A Mercedes pulled up, and I glanced away, looking toward the street and picking some crumbs out of my braces.

A black family emerged from the car, and I sat up a little straighter then, taking my hand out of my mouth. The father, I presumed, popped the trunk and began pulling things out. The back door opened and a young man got out of the car. His skin reminded me of my daddy's – it was like that nasty ass candy you'd find in the bottom of your grandmother's purse. Werther's. I disdained that candy as much as I disdained my daddy.

I was snatched from my reverie when I heard the boy's mother call out to me. She'd managed to make it to the bottom of the steps and smiled up at me. "First year?" she asked.

I nodded and swung my legs over to the steps, before I walked down and put my hands in the back pockets of my jean shorts. My curves had only recently emerged, near the end of my junior year. I was left with a body I was still growing into.

"Just moved in."

She smiled and folded her arms. "Where are you from?"

"Wisconsin," I said. "My mom is flying back in a little."

"Will you stop prying?" the boy asked, as he came from behind the car, with a box cradled beneath his arm. "Always getting in somebody's business."

The annoyance in his voice didn't match the stoic face he wore. I smiled a little and blushed beneath my deeply pigmented cheeks. My eyes traced the boy as he stood in front of us – athletic build with hair that settled into a soft s-curl, like his lips then.

"Excuse me, don't be rude. Introduce yourself," his mother said to him.

"Jacob," he said. He glanced at me, or *through* me – I couldn't tell the difference then.

Jacob's father locked the car and came around carrying a bag. "Let's get inside. Do you have dinner plans?" his mother asked.

"I'm planning to explore a little. I'm fine," I said.

"Well enjoy your walk. With your family being so far away, please call us if you need anything. We aren't too far." She smiled and placed her hand on my shoulder.

My heart swelled with gratitude at this black momma, offering to mother a child that wasn't her own. As I watched the three of them ascend the steps, a feeling of longing swept over me. I forced a smile, before I turned and studied my surroundings. The tall, stately brick buildings were accented with white columns and double hung windows. Vines strangled the campus – covered lamp posts, snaked up the sides of buildings.

I'd selected Monroe University for a few reasons: they had a strong journalism program and they were recently at the center of a national conversation on race after a black student started an online independent magazine. *By Any Means*, also known as *BAM,* was a compilation of student submissions detailing microaggressions and racial violence across campus. Like the vines, racism strangled this campus and black students weaponized their stories.

To write was to resist.

To write was to exist. I wanted to write, but my desire to document wasn't rooted in the black intellectual tradition. I hadn't read Baldwin or Du Bois at eighteen. But I had watched Oscar Grant die face down in Oakland. I saw Trayvon's face on hooded black boys in passing. I experienced exposure and erasure in the Midwest. I revered writing as much as I revered blackness. A black writer was like a mortician, tending to the forgotten and preserving the black corporal shell and it's suffering. To write was to live. There were times when I could've turned my back on blackness, but I ran toward it instead.

CHAPTER 2.

A short walk turned into a self-guided tour of the surrounding city. I use city lightly, for its size would best be described as a town. Monroe was a small, private liberal arts school. It was situated about thirty miles outside of Providence, Rhode Island and despite its relatively progressive bearings, I knew that there were different shades of liberal. Before I committed to attending, I dug through the university's archives online. Monroe had an interesting history.

During the height of the Civil Rights Movement, the university was a hotbed for student resistance. In 1967, fifteen black students occupied the president's office with a number of demands, including a diversified teaching staff and a black cultural center. The black cultural center was granted, but the other issues were enduring and difficult to address long after the protests ended. Writers at *By Any Means* recently released a new list of demands from black and brown students. The complaints were hauntingly similar to their predecessors'.

Based on photos I'd seen in the archives, Monroe retained much of its original architecture. The buildings were beautiful, large and intimidating. Many were under construction as the university restored them. Monroe valued tradition and this was clear, but I wondered if that was a good thing.

On the other side of College Avenue, there were quaint antique shops and cafes. I caught a glimpse of my reflection in the windows that I passed and noted the stark contrast between my skin and the locals. My Madison upbringing had prepared me for this. *Other* didn't feel so strange anymore.

When I returned to my residence hall, I crossed the threshold to find a short, stocky brunette standing in the lobby. She wore a university half-zip with a matching water bottle in her hand.

"You must be Nia!"

I raised an eyebrow. There were more than fifty girls on my floor, but this girl knew who I was? I nodded apprehensively and studied her.

"I'm Elise. I'll be your resident advisor this year. We have a slight switch in room assignments so I wanted to catch you."

"Switch in room assignments?" I smacked my lips. I was already annoyed at the thought of having to move my shit – I just got here!

"Olivia requested a room on another floor, so she won't be with you this year," Elise said as she stuck out her bottom lip for pity, I suppose. I didn't need any.

I raised my eyebrows as far as they could go. "...So who will I be rooming with?" I tapped my foot lightly and held my arms crossed. Elise smiled a little but as the uneasiness brewed between us, her face grew red.

"So that's the good news – you'll get to have your own space. At least for this semester," she said.

My eyes fell to her Birkenstocks. She was shorter than me and she pushed her hair behind her ear almost incessantly. I tilted my head to the side to get a better look at her. The words that I wanted to say climbed up into my throat and sat there burning with anticipation. I parted my lips and blurted the first thing that came to mind:

"She moved 'cause I'm black."

Elise's face swept over with horror. "No, nothing like that." She shook her head and put her hands out to establish the distance between the two of us. "It was really a matter of preference."

"Preference...right," I said softly. "Thanks for the heads up, Elise. It'll be a great year." I matched her smile and intertwined my fingers to hide my shaking hands.

"I'll see you at the floor meeting!"

She placed a hand on my shoulder before she walked off down the hall. I allowed my eyes to follow her, before I noticed that my heart was nearly beating out of my chest.

My initial interaction with Elise set the precedent and our relationship never recovered.

***

Floor meetings were the bane of my existence. I established that early and stopped attending. At the first meeting, Elise introduced herself and asked all of us to share something unique about ourselves. I quickly took stock of who was in the room before it was my turn.

"I'm the only person of color on this floor."

Elise stumbled. She attempted to build bridges between the rest of the residents and me; a worthy effort, but one that I didn't really engage. When I stopped attending the floor meetings, Elise didn't bother to confront me.

Racial tension reared its big, ubiquitous head immediately. On multiple occasions my hair was a conversation starter, and propriety didn't matter to folks around here. Fingers found their way into my hair during brief interactions and short quips about things my "fro resembled" had my white counterparts tickled. Under the guise of friendliness, they unknowingly exposed themselves for who they really were.

The first few weeks proved to be more difficult for me than I'd imagined. I spoke to my mother more than three times each day and found myself reviewing the transfer application process for University of Wisconsin – or anywhere closer to home than here.

I attempted to capture all of my encounters with words. I'd gotten through an entire journal that first month, for the encounters were more frequent than I could fathom. One Friday after my shower, I sat my hair products on one of the sinks in the communal bathroom. I took a deep breath and glanced at the smattering of products before me. We only had a drugstore on campus, so I grabbed what I could. I picked up anything that said "natural" or "textured."

I scooped out a handful of leave-in conditioner and rubbed it between my palms like I'd seen the girls do on YouTube. I distributed it through my strands before I applied coconut oil, followed by curl cream. I stared at the saturated hair in the mirror for a while and smacked my lips. I tossed my hands up and decided to quit for the day. I washed my hands and changed the rubber bands for my braces. I hoped that my hair would curl – even if it were just a little.

A girl from my floor emerged from one of the stalls and began to wash her hands. I didn't even know she was in there. She looked over at my things before her eyes traveled up to my hair.

"Wow, that's a lot of stuff," she said.

She studied my short, saturated afro and I sent her a chilly look through the mirror. I prepared myself for a joke and got ready to fire back.

"Does it make your hair curl up?"

I shrugged. "Water does that. This just helps the curl stay moisturized, I suppose. I'm new to this."

"New to what?" She continued to probe.

"To being natural. I cut my hair recently."

"Oh, I see," she said.

Her tone indicated that she was relatively familiar with the language but her curiosity didn't stop there. She was staring at it like she had something else to ask. If my body language hadn't made it clear that I was done talking, I figured my face would.

"Can I...touch it? I've been really curious and didn't want to just reach up there."

"No. I just washed it."

I looked over at her in disbelief. This was the third time this week!

"My hands are clean!" she joked.

I didn't know this girl – I mean I *really* didn't know this girl! An occasional conversation over toothpaste didn't equate to a friendship.

"Maybe next time," I said, appeasing her. I even accented the statement with a smile.

"Good luck with it!" she said before she bounced out of the bathroom. I rolled my eyes to Mars before I looked at the door and became tempted to lock it. No more distractions.

***

Finding community here was key – but I'd only run into a handful of black students since the start of the semester. I had an English class with a few, and the three of them seemed to know each other. I wanted to join them, but my tardiness was a tough habit to break. Each time I arrived to the lecture hall for English, all of the seats near the black students were gone.

Our professor's research focus was literature by women of color and although she was not a woman of color, I registered for the course because of her. Standing at the top of the lecture hall, Dr. Ames cleared her throat and scanned the room. Most days, I found her class engaging and when we started reading Toni Morrison's *Sula*, I stayed up and finished the book in one night.

"Let's do a temperature check. Thoughts on the book?" Silence followed.

I looked around the room and imagined that my hand was glued to the desk. I could *not* be the only person to share – or even the first. Not today. A hand rose in the back of the room, and I turned around to see a fair skinned girl – one of the black students – waiting to contribute.

"Part of me was rooting for Sula, honestly. She was a complex character. Maybe polarizing, but there was a lot of truth in her contempt. The people of The Bottom used her as a reference – they defined their goodness against what they perceived to be her evil. What is goodness? And what is rotten or unworthy, if its all relative?"

I studied the girl while she finished her remarks, before I turned to look at Dr. Ames who nodded and pursed her lips. "That's a great contribution, Cecilia. Thank you. What are other thoughts?"

When she was met with the familiar silence that defined this unengaged group of freshmen, she clapped loudly and stepped forward in the room. "I've noticed a divide in the class, so today we'll mix things up. Let's get everyone involved," she stated as she walked up and down the aisles.

I turned my head toward the black students to find that they were already looking at me. The four of us exchanged glances and small smiles. Dr. Ames proceeded to place us in small groups, and as expected, none of the black students were in the same group.

The students in my group craned their necks to stare at me when I sat down to join them. Dr. Ames circled the room and listened in on conversations. A few students bemoaned the centering of race, but most of the group struggled to offer anything insightful. The most they could offer were complaints about the use of African American Vernacular English, and the narrative's structure.

"The lack of engagement with this text is telling," I stated. I sat back in the chair and sighed.

Dr. Ames folded her arms and studied the reaction of the group. Many of them looked away, but the others stared with little to offer in response. I looked up at Dr. Ames, and hoped she'd provide some guidance – *or* check this group. Something.

"Tell us more, Nia."

"Students in this class have tackled more challenging narratives, and lauded authors who weren't women of color – authors who were arguably less skilled than Toni Morrison. I just think these critiques are lazy. There are universal themes in this text – like those offered by Cecilia – that could be considered by anyone. I don't think people are willing to connect to Toni's work because of who she is."

My comment was disregarded. The group continued with lazy critiques and any challenge or rebuttal was met with a shrug. After I'd said enough to earn my participation points for the day, I checked out of the conversation.

Near the end of class, while students were finishing up their conversations, Dr. Ames invited me to speak with her after but I declined. "I'm fine, really. This isn't new – I'm used to being one of few."

"Well where are you from?" Dr. Ames probed.

"No disrespect Dr. Ames, but does that even matter?" I asked her.

As I gathered my things and students left the classroom, the black students approached me. I looked up to find them studying me curiously. There were three of them, each with a smirk and a desire to connect. We waited for Dr. Ames to leave the hall before we fell out with raucous laughter. The four of us cackled like we were all in on a joke; like we understood that sometimes, laughter was the only thing that could hold us together.

"Everyday we sit and wait to see if you'll be here on time so that you can sit next to us. We've tried saving you a seat but we've gotten complaints." An eye roll sealed the sentence before she smiled and stuck out her hand. "I'm Lauren."

"I'm Nia." I smiled warmly at the other two.

"I'm Cecilia. Your hair is so pretty." Her eyes bounced between my hair and my face, and for the first time since I arrived, I felt that the compliment was genuine. Her thick, manicured eyebrows rose and fell and my eyes went to her silky black hair, worn in a messy bun on the top of her head.

"Thanks for sharing in class today," I said to her.

"I'm Jordan." The last student swung his backpack over his shoulder. "Are you heading to the Black Student Union's barbecue?"

"I didn't know about it."

Lauren invited me to join them and I jumped at the chance. I followed them out of the English building and as I walked next to them, I thought, *maybe I could survive here.* Despite our visibility – despite the contrast – there was power in numbers. As we walked, we processed our English class. We agreed that the four of us would sit together, despite Dr. Ames' effort to integrate the class. We armed ourselves with each other and became a barricade.

I could hear music and smell charcoal the closer I got to the Black Cultural Center. My heart raced as I turned the corner and saw the crowd of students congregating behind the center. A group of older black girls, adorned with Greek letters, walked by and I marveled at the sight of them.

"Are you 4a?" I heard.

"No I'm a freshman," I responded.

Cecilia chuckled. "Your hair type, girl."

"Hair type? I'm not familiar."

"Did you just do the big chop?"

"Right before school," I nodded.

"What dorm are you in? I never see you outside of class. Most of us know each other," she said, as she waved at students that we passed.

"I live in Mark Hall. We don't have any black students – just one other boy, but he and I don't see each other," I said.

"I live in the African American Learning Community with Lauren and Jordan. Come meet some people."

I followed her and surveyed the barbecue. There were students all over the lawn, engaging in conversation, eating, and dancing. From time to time, I could hear the DJ make announcements about upcoming events, as thick bass lines filled the air. The heat was abnormally sweltering for late September – like an Indian summer – but the students welcomed the sun's rays. I plopped my bag down at a table next to Cecilia, and met seven sets of eyes.

"This is my new friend Nia," Cecilia announced.

"Cici! Stop bringing home strays!" One boy yelled.

The table responded with laughter, and I smiled large and wide, until my mouth felt too big for my face. Like vultures, the students devoured me with questions.

"Where have you been?"

"Did you get stuck with a white roommate?"

"How do you know Cecilia?"

The focus of the table shifted when a male student entered the barbecue. The entire table went quiet as he walked across the grass toward the food table. I watched him as he shook hands with students and grew comfortable in the space. His walk was smooth, almost like a glide.

"Is that him?" Lauren asked.

I turned around to see her pointing in his direction. Jordan confirmed with a head nod. "Yeah that's him."

"Who?" I was the first to ask.

"That's Quentin, the one who started that magazine online."

"*By Any Means*?" I asked.

The students nodded in sync and continued to watch him. I picked up on the conversations at the table about him. He was a fourth-year student studying business, or *something*. According to unconfirmed sources, administration was threatening to pull his scholarship because of the magazine. It had national readership, and Quentin refused to take it down. Also unconfirmed – he was single.

I grabbed my empty cup and headed toward the cooler to grab another soda. Quentin had completed his rounds and retired at the cooler as I opened the can and poured the soda in my cup. I looked over at him and took a sip. His skin resembled mine, and he had beautiful white teeth set in a mouth sculpted by God himself. His broad shoulders peaked through the fitted shirt he wore, and I thought that he was the most handsome man I'd ever seen. His eyes traveled to me, and when he noticed me staring, he smiled reflexively. I stumbled with embarrassment and tossed the can into the nearest trash.

"Sorry," I said.

He shook his head. "No worries."

I looked down at the cup in my hand and then out at the grass while I searched for words. I was interested in writing for *By Any Means*, but I hadn't the slightest clue of how to articulate that.

"I'm a huge fan of your writing. Long-time subscriber." I smiled a little and Quentin's ears perked, before he looked over at me with curiosity sewn into his brow. His lips parted and he turned toward me. My heart rate increased when his cologne filled my nose, leaving me slightly dizzy. *Maybe it's the heat*, I thought.

"Do you write?" he asked.

I nodded. "I do."

"I started a writing collective on campus, you should join us. Come by if you can."

He pulled a card out of his wallet and handed it to me, before he placed his hand on my arm. "We'd really like to see you." he said, before he walked off and disappeared into the crowd.

CHAPTER 3.

I was a notebook writer. Before I cut my hair I was writing in every margin of a tattered leather-bound notebook my daddy gifted me years earlier for Christmas. I scribbled down the mind's musings. Writing was a place of refuge for me, and often the only way I could glean some clarity from life's trials. Pages were full of names and mascara stains, dates and dirt. The dirt wasn't fertile though. I didn't believe that anything beautiful could ever spring from it.

So I ripped out most of the pages.

The night that I took Quentin up on his offer to join the writing collective, I clutched what was left of the notebook and watched him get settled in. He was the president of an organization called Victory through Verse. The group met weekly for writing workshops, with the opportunity to be published in a chapbook each semester. Quentin's hands rested in his tapered khaki pants as he stood in the middle of a borrowed classroom. Sitting there in that cramped room full of restless poets and writers, my eyes traced his frame as he walked back and forth and introduced the group's purpose and goals for the year.

"Let's do a warm up," he said.

His voice took on a particular cadence in this setting, one that was characteristic of spoken word poets. With much practice, Quentin could extend his voice to every inch of the room and it draped our ears like silk. I leaned forward and waited for instructions.

"I want you to list three words that describe how you've felt in the last year," he said. "I want you to write with your soul," he cooed.

I stared at my open notebook and imagined a blinking cursor at the top of a page. Three words came to mind, and before I could censor myself, I threw them on the page without judgment.

Raw – Hollow – Malleable

We were asked to complete a free write, and words circled in my mind as phrases assembled and disassembled. A few ideas emerged, and I skipped down to the middle of the page. Words began to spill out of my pen in purple ink.

When Quentin asked for a volunteer I sank in my seat and shut my notebook. Quentin's eyes scanned the room before they fell on me. I glanced at him then to find a small smile on his face. He held a steady gaze.

"I don't want to call anyone out," he said softly.

He and I managed a staring contest – there, in the middle of the room. I sat up then and pushed my lips to the side, tapping my pen lightly and looking around to see if anyone was planning to go first.

"I'll go," I blurted.

Quentin's smile reduced to a smirk and he leaned forward and rested his elbows on his knees. "Please," he said, as he dropped his head and shut his eyes. I took a deep breath in and allowed the air to settle in my expanding lungs.

"I'm sorry, I'm a little nervous."

"No disclaimers, sis." I heard someone say.

I stopped picking flowers –
My mother would slap my raw, fresh hands,
Her lips pursed with disapproval.

"When you pick them – they die," she'd say.
I ventured further – wanting to test her words.
Spring after spring, I'd pull flowers from the soil responsible for their beauty.

They did die – like most beautiful things.
An innocent affinity for beauty; the trauma of truth.

I never flowered.
Emerged a strange fruit instead.
Planted with seeds of self-loathe,
Of a deprived body – I grew among the weeds.

Grateful to finally be pulled,

To be yanked from the roots,
His soiled hands a troublesome mistake,
Mistook for sun.

When I started the poem, my voice shook but grew more stable as I moved through, line by line. Quentin lifted his head and allowed his eyes to crawl all over me.

When I finished, I shut the notebook and looked down – I couldn't bring my eyes up from the floor. Soft snaps filtered into my ears, and timidly, I looked up to meet smiles of affirmation throughout the room. My back straightened and pride danced up my spine. I sat back slowly in my chair and looked over at Quentin. "Thank you," he mouthed.

Another hand rose with trepidation and Quentin turned to them. "Please share."

***

The leaves were the first things to change. I sat in front of a window and studied the trees that surrounded campus. At a coffee shop only a few paces from the university's gate, the smell of chai and coffee beans nestled beneath my nose. It was Sunday – the Lord's Day – but I hadn't been to church since I left home.

I took a sip of the overpriced latte I'd bought and attempted to refocus, before my attention drifted elsewhere. The chimes above the door sounded, and I turned then, curious to see who'd walked in. Quentin was looking toward me with a backpack on. I turned back toward the window, hoping he hadn't seen me see him.

He headed to the counter and I allowed my back to curl toward my book. Coltrane's horn blared in my ears as I grabbed my pen to highlight another sentence. The words were beginning to blur the longer I sat there. Quentin's cologne greeted me before he did. He pulled out the stool next to me and settled in. We shared a cramped counter space as he poured a pack of sugar in his cup. He looked ahead, stirring his coffee rhythmically. I allowed my eyes to travel from his hands to his face, before I took out an ear bud and shared the view with him.

"Never would've guessed that you were a poet," he said.

"I'm not. I just write."

"Well you're a wordsmith. How long have you been writing?"

"Since I've had words to describe how I feel."

Quentin tested the temperature of his coffee while he watched cars pass. My palms were sweating as the silence brewed between us. If it weren't for the coffee beans, his cologne would've strangled me – smothered me with its sweet smell. I glanced over at him to find his eyes anchoring in mine.

"I can usually get a lot of writing done in the fall. Best time of year for an introvert." He smiled a little and turned back to his coffee, resuming the mindless stirring. "Have you been writing lately?"

"A little. Classes have gotten in the way. How's your semester?"

"Fine," he responded. "I'm keeping up better than before. Sometimes I feel like I'm a hamster on a wheel, though. Just running for nothing."

His voice was soft and low, and as his breath left his mouth, it created a small circle of condensation on the window in front of us. He turned a little, allowing his knee to make contact with mine. My heart fluttered and I noticed a small tattoo on his wrist as he lifted his hand to take another sip.

LIVE.

"What does your tattoo mean?"

He looked down at it with a curious glance, almost like he'd forgotten it was there. He tripped over the word before he put his other hand over it and looked at me. "Maybe I'll tell you someday."

The space between us shrunk the longer he and I sat there. We watched the colors of the leaves blend and smear, turning into colorful smudges when the rain started.

"I think you were right about the fall," I said finally.

"I like the idea of starting over. And the part of it that requires you to shed," he said.

"I know something about that." I smiled and nodded.

His eyes went to my hair. "When did you cut your hair?"

"Right before school."

"Were you choosing to shed for school or for another reason?" He took his last sip of his coffee and sat the empty cup down on the counter in front of us. He draped his arm casually on the back of my stool.

"Another reason," I said.

My voice was a hint above a whisper then, as I watched the rain drops merge and separate and merge again on the window. The sound of spoons hitting plates, rain hitting the ground and fingers on keyboards streamed into my ears on a constant loop, while Quentin fixed his lips to ask another question.

"What could've made you part with your strands?" he asked.

I wanted to say that the pain that I carried was insidious enough to drive my hair away but I settled for something else – something lighter.

"It was breaking off. I was under a lot of stress," I said.

Stress. I'd managed to reduce my pain to that, but I wasn't convincing. Quentin's curious eyes curled around me like he was searching for the truth crouching behind my gaze, but he didn't probe. He placed his hand on my knee and offered a warm smile. We continued that way for a while, and I didn't want it to end.

Neither of us knew this then, but that afternoon at the coffee shop, our hearts braced themselves for the shape of a season we hadn't accounted for. We were not the fall, but he and I would have to shed.

***

If I had to describe Quentin in one word, it would be **elusive**. There would be moments of understanding, followed by complete and utter confusion. He was a conundrum – a code that I was committed to cracking. I showed up to Victory through Verse every week, looking for a trace of the man I'd met at the coffee shop. After our conversation that Sunday, he retreated to a space of unfamiliarity that felt cold and distant.

I lingered one Monday with the intention of asking about *By Any Means*. This week, Quentin's glasses sat perched on his nose, and when I approached him after the meeting, he took them off and put them on the desk in front of him.

"I don't think you're ready for *BAM*."

I was taken aback. He hadn't read any of my writing outside of my responses to the creative prompts in our workshops. I studied every issue of *By Any Means*. And since I arrived, I kept a record of racial encounters on campus – both overt and covert. I was ready to write for him.

When I shared this with him, he smiled and shrugged.

"I'm not concerned about the writing, Nia."

Writers in the magazine were often subject to scrutiny, isolation and in some instances, violence. Since its inception, *By Any Means* had lost a number of its writers after they chose to transfer to other institutions. Quentin packed up his laptop and I stood before him, attempting to plead my case.

"I can write under a pseudonym," I offered.

Quentin stopped packing up and looked up at me before he sat on the desk and considered the idea. "What would it be?"

"Brown Girl?"

"…Let's sleep on it. I don't want you to be harmed by this in any way. It's not hard to have your experience at Monroe tarnished by something this incendiary. I got the president down my back. Even the chief diversity officer is trying to get me to quit."

His face stretched with discomfort as he recalled conversations in offices with locked doors, death threats in his inbox, and letters sent home to his mother in Chicago. I stood and listened as his stream of speech slowed to a low murmur.

"It's getting late," he said.

I gripped the straps of my backpack and turned on my heels to leave. "Well keep me in mind. I'm not intimidated."

"You should be, but I admire your bravery." He chuckled.

He followed me out of the classroom and turned off the light before he inquired about my walk. Mark Hall was on the other side of campus and Quentin scoffed at the idea of me walking alone this late. When he offered to join me, I obliged. Our walk to my dorm was pretty quiet.

As fall settled in, nighttime brought the cold. The two of us clutched our sleeves as the wind whistled and howled and shimmied across our bodies. My mind was crawling with questions that I wanted to ask but as we neared my residence hall, the words had only managed to fall at the back of my tongue. I was too shy to ask him anything.

We stopped at the corner and turned toward each other. Quentin blew into his hands and looked up and down the street. His hypervigilance was apparent and provided a cloak of protection as the two of us stood beneath a large maple tree with leaves the color of rust.

"I'll call you about *By Any Means*. I need your number though."

My hands trembled in the cold as I pulled out my cell phone and handed it over to him. He grabbed my cold hand with his free hand as he typed his number into my phone. His thumb swiped across the back of my hand, and I allowed my fingers to curl around his. The only light we could discern was a distant lamppost and the cell phone as it shone on his face. He slipped my phone back into my pocket before he reached for a hug. The embrace lasted longer than I expected, but he quickly disappeared into the dark.

An elusive departure.

At least he was consistent.

CHAPTER 4.

If I could have any superpower, it would be invisibility. My melanin made that hard at Monroe, so I became avoidant instead.

I burrowed inside of my residence hall and moved with stealth and in silence. I showered earlier than the rest of the floor and slipped out for dinner before I was asked to join. Weeks had gone by and I hadn't said more than a few words to the students around me.

I rarely saw Jacob, the other black student in my hall. Occasionally, I'd catch a glimpse of him turning a corner or leaving out with his floor mates. The few times that our eyes managed to meet, my smile was met with general apathy and the casual head nod. I never saw him with students of color but he didn't seem to feel out of place.

On Friday nights, I usually found comfort in my loneliness. Some food – usually from the Italian restaurant around the corner or the local pizza spot on College Avenue – and my music created the space I needed to write. A knock at the door one evening startled me, and I turned down my music to see if it was for me. When I heard the knock again, I parted with my laptop and slid into some flip-flops. I looked through the peephole to find Jacob there and stood back a little bit. *What the hell does he want,* I thought.

"One second!" I shrieked.

I pretended to be too busy to open the door, but stood and attempted to fix my face. I didn't want to look excited but he was my first visitor! I settled for a slight scowl and pulled the door ajar.

"Hey," I said, as I sighed with indifference.

Jacob studied me, his eyes shielded by a Yankees baseball cap that he wore low, in the middle of his forehead. His hands rested comfortably in tapered sweatpants before he swiped his thumb across his lips.

"Want to grab some ice cream at the dairy?" he asked.

I narrowed my eyes before I nodded. "Let me get my wallet,"

I left the door open while he waited in the hall. He studied my space, noticing the empty side of the room. "You got the room to yourself, huh?"

"Not by choice," I yelled out to him, as I dug around looking for my wallet.

I'd converted the other bed into a couch and filled it with pillows. Although the makeshift couch was rarely used, the empty mattress before it was an eyesore. There were posters lining the walls of artists I'd seen in concert and others that I'd inherited from my mother. Davis, Coltrane, Monk – the soundtrack to my childhood. Jacob furrowed his brow.

"What do you know about jazz?" he asked, peaking his head into the room now.

"What do you mean? I play the piano and my mom used to play jazz at the house all of the time."

"I play the trumpet," he responded.

I draped my cross-body purse over my shoulder before the two of us left to head to the dairy. I bombarded him with questions about his semester and his life before Monroe. He answered them all with short responses and a lackadaisical disposition.

He grew up in Massachusetts. His parents were Harvard graduates. His mother, a gynecologist with her own practice, and his father a professor at Boston University. That was the most that I could manage to get from him. I didn't understand Jacob – he invited me out for ice cream but acted like he didn't want to talk. I figured that this was more about who he was and less about me and decided not to take it personal.

"What makes you smile?" I asked him.

I looked at him curiously as we sat across from each other at a table outside of the dairy. We were the last customers to be served, and other undergraduates swept around us as they prepared to close for the night.

"That's a weird question," he said.

He licked his lips and gathered more ice cream on his spoon. He'd settled for vanilla while I got two flavors – salted caramel and chocolate chunk. His broad shoulders slumped forward with ease, and as we sat there, he dodged eye contact like a professional. Silence fell upon us and Jacob looked around at the empty tables.

"A lot of things – a lot of things make me smile," he said.

"So, why'd you invite me for ice cream?" I licked my spoon like a child and watched him prepare an answer.

"My mother asked about you the other day and I realized we hadn't hung out yet, so..."

I raised an eyebrow and smiled a little. *Yeah okay*, I thought. I didn't know him but I felt that there was more to his invitation this evening. Jacob's eyes fell on the table and his ice cream became soupy as he stared at nothing in particular. I scraped the sides of my cup of ice cream. There wasn't much left and I figured the short outing would end sooner if I appeared finished. To my surprise, Jacob's lips parted once more.

"So I'm running for a position with student government, right?" he started.

I nodded, still licking my spoon.

"Someone wrote nigger on one of the campaign posters outside of Wright Hall," he said.

My eyes flew up to his face and he and I made eye contact for the first time this evening. He stared a hole through my head, waiting for me to react. When I responded with a chuckle and shook my head, Jacob inquired about what my thoughts were.

"I don't...I don't know. Are you planning to continue?" I asked.

"I'm withdrawing from the campaign," he said.

"Don't let them scare you off. This campus needs a brown face up there."

He smiled. "Well, why don't you run?"

"I'm not in the business of occupying spaces like USG."

"What kinds of spaces are those?"

"Ones where representation is a campaign platform and diversity is a strategy."

"But you came to Monroe – a predominantly white school?" he challenged.

"I have my reasons."

I allowed the words to hang in the air before a thought came to mind: *there was a story here*. I looked around the empty dairy and leaned in toward Jacob.

"...Let me write about it," I said.

Jacob contested. He was one of the only black students running for student government and he didn't want to be at the center of any *race war*, he called it.

"It wouldn't be a race war!"

"I just don't think that's a good idea, Nia. I want to run for office, make an impact, and make some connections. I don't want to be the *black* vice president – just the vice president."

His words stung. I paused a little and gathered my thoughts.

"But you're black Jacob and someone is trying to remind you of that. Your story matters more than you think. Let me write about it."

He ignored me, changing the subject. He seemed contemplative but we moved to lighter topics. When he finished his soupy ice cream, the two of us headed back to the dorm. I was burning with ideas – different angles, different approaches to his story. Jacob smiled a little and looked around as the two of us walked together.

"It was weird. When I saw the flyer, I realized that I didn't have anyone to talk to about how I felt. I didn't even call my dad. I just let it fester all day until I started snapping on my roommates. That's when I came downstairs to meet you."

"Why me?" I asked. Jacob and I hadn't spoken since I met him in front of the residence hall.

"…I figured you might understand," he said softly.

"How did you feel when you saw the flyer?"

"…Like I was burning from the inside. I want to fight back, but it's like I'm swinging at a ghost…or Goliath."

"I think racism feels like that," I said.

We got to the dorm and the two of us stood across from each other on the steps. We were hesitant to head inside with so many words left unsaid. I looked out toward the darkened street and Jacob watched me. His head dropped and he wiped his hand over his face, before he said what he figured he might regret.

"Where would you publish it?" he asked.

A smile filled my face and the text to Quentin wrote itself.

I've got a story.

***

We shared a table at the library. My leg bounced with anticipation while

Quentin reviewed my piece on Jacob. He made a few edits before he looked over the laptop at me. Until this point, he'd only raised an eyebrow and twisted his lips to the side once or twice. With each indentation in his forehead, I perspired. My fear of his disapproval was apparent and when he looked up at me finally his mouth cracked open with a chuckle.

"Why are you afraid? This is great."

He pushed the laptop back, before he slid down in the chair and rested his head on the back of the upholstered chair he sat in. His hands ran up and down the worn arms while he tossed a few ideas around. He shrugged finally, and leant forward, resting his elbows on the table. He agreed to this first piece being published, but didn't make any promises about future features. I published under Brown Girl to protect my identity – and Jacob's name was omitted to protect his.

"When will this be done?" I asked.

"I release every other Thursday," he said.

Quentin pushed open the door of the library and we walked out onto the steps just as the rain started. I smacked my lips and reached around for my umbrella, to find an empty pocket instead. Quentin tugged at the strings on his hoodie before he saw the anguish on my face. He placed his backpack on the step and pulled the hoodie above his head, before he handed it to me. I looked down at it, and then at him before I shook my head in refusal. He continued to hold the temporary covering until I took it. The rain poured and accumulated in small puddles across the quad. Completely unprepared for the trek, I draped myself in Quentin's hoodie and tossed him an appreciative smile before I sprinted back to my dorm.

The scent in Quentin's hoodie lingered for days despite the rain. I hung it up near the door to dry, and each subsequent afternoon when I returned from class, the scent hit me and made me smile.

Cecilia trailed behind me after English one afternoon when she saw the hoodie hanging in my room. She raised an eyebrow before she put down her bag and sat on my makeshift sofa.

After we met in class, Cecilia and I quickly grew close. Our budding friendship was aided by our mutual love for black literature, but it honestly stood on our shared cynicism. We were critical of the world around us, and we didn't feel like we had to be anyone else around each other. She was multiracial, but aligned most with her Creole heritage. A curly-headed rebel raised by a white mother in a small suburb outside of Hartford? She had a lot of stories.

"I always knew that I was different and I needed my mother to acknowledge that," she said while she lied on my bed, with her upper half draping over the side.

Like we often did, we fell into a conversation about our identities, and how we had to reconcile who we were with where we'd come from.

"...You were fighting for your differences to be recognized, and I was hoping to blend, hoping to feel beautiful," I said.

"Hoping to feel beautiful? You're a queen." She snapped her fingers and rolled her neck.

"Sometimes you try too hard Cici," I mumbled.

When my phone vibrated on my desk, I sat up to grab it. At the sight of Quentin's name, my heart raced and my palms grew moist. Cecilia noted the change in my face and pursed her lips.

"Who's that?" she asked.

"Quentin. He...wants to pick up his hoodie?"

I looked over at her and she allowed her eyebrows to rise before she looked down at her phone and shrugged a little.

"I thought you two hung out all of the time. Why are you so weird right now?"

"We don't hang out, technically. I'm writing a piece for his magazine."

"I didn't know he was picking up freshmen to write for him."

"I don't think it's common. I just had a good story."

"Well I guess I'll head back to the slums. The buses stop running after a certain hour because we're in the hood."

Cecilia's affinity for the African American Learning Community went south when students realized that the residence hall was rife with issues. Bug infestations, water outages and isolation from the rest of the campus were among the biggest concerns detailed in a recent exposé written for *By Any Means*. She gathered her things and lingered for a moment.

"Be safe," she said softly.

We locked eyes and something stirred between us.

"Always," I said. She left, leaving her words at the door.

I waited a few moments to respond to Quentin's text, before I changed out of my clothes and tidied up the room. When Quentin arrived he parked on an adjacent corner at a meter and strolled across the street. With his arrival text sent to me, he walked up the steps and studied the building's architecture. The door opened and I stood there with a sour face.

"What's wrong with you?" He chuckled.

"It's cold, c'mon!"

He came inside and as he followed me, he studied the Halloween and Thanksgiving decorations that covered the walls. Mark Hall was notably different. When he was a freshman, Quentin realized that Monroe's race problem was structural. Even the dorms were segregated. As he strolled the hall behind me, he spun his keys around his finger and furrowed his brow.

"How'd you end up living in Mark?" he asked.

"Because of my scholarship, why?"

"I've never actually been inside of his dorm," he said.

I unlocked the door to my room and stood in the foyer to grab his hoodie. When I turned around, he was nosily craning his neck to see my room.

"What, I can't come in?" he asked.

"I didn't know if you wanted to."

"I paid to park," he said as he walked in.

Hearing his deep voice bounce off of the walls in my room was jarring. He removed his shoes with respect, before he walked onto the carpet and surveyed my space. A manicured beard framed Quentin's chin, and as he stood there, he nuzzled the beard with his fingers. I sat down on my bed and looked at anything but him, while he thumbed through my books and read titles aloud. He picked one up and smiled to himself.

"What'd you grab?" I asked. He turned the book toward me – *Sister Outsider* by Audre Lorde.

"I love the quote about the tyrannies we swallow. That what we keep inside can ultimately become our master. We learn to suffer in silence and allow it to rule us. Sometimes without noticing."

"Why that quote?" I asked him.

"It's the reason I started *By Any Means*. I felt like I wanted to scream. And so I did."

He put the book back and turned toward me, before he swung his arms back and forth. The space in the room seemed to shrink and I went to grab a bottle of water to cool off. I handed him one and resumed my spot on the edge of the bed, while Quentin got comfortable across from me. He took a sip of his water and his eyes danced up my legs to my face. We met eyes and he smiled a little.

"I'm bringing you on as a staff writer for the magazine," he said.

"Me? I thought you were apprehensive about me writing for you."

"I was and I am. But I'm less apprehensive and more intrigued by you."

"What's intriguing about me?"

"I can't read you."

"I don't understand," I said.

Quentin twisted his lips up and to the side, before he leaned forward and rested his elbows on his knees. "In the time that we've spent together, I've found that when it comes to *you*, you have little to say. You could write a diatribe on racism in intercollegiate sports but couldn't bear to utter more than a few dozen words about Nia."

"What does that have to do with writing for this magazine?"

"Everything. It has everything to do with writing. Period."

"I know who I am."

"Do you?" he challenged. "Why did you start writing?"

"I had to," I responded.

"*Why*, Nia?"

I folded my arms and folded into myself, while I searched the floor for words that weren't there. I shrugged. "I felt like I had to…like I was bursting at the seams. My pain, my own shit and our collective trauma had me feeling like I could implode at any moment. So I just started writing everything down, studying my surroundings and trying to find meaning in it all."

"That's it?" he inquired.

"I don't know what answer you're looking for," I said.

Quentin smirked. "You'll crack eventually."

CHAPTER 5.

In our writing together, we were knee-deep in pain, trudging through the muck and mire of injustice, and searching for some resolution far in the distance. A worthy effort, indeed.

The initial piece on Jacob was wildly successful, leading Quentin to bring me on as a staff writer and assistant editor. Jacob's party won the student election, and he assumed his role as the vice president for the Undergraduate Student Government. He and I hadn't crossed paths since I interviewed him for the story, but he sent a small message of appreciation via text.

Over the next few months, Quentin and I spent an inordinate amount of time together reviewing submissions for *By Any Means*. Late into the evening we would read submissions, write papers for classes and study for exams. I imagined that my makeshift sofa had adopted his scent by now, so I didn't bother to clean the sheets. Quentin's eyes followed my bare legs as I paced my dorm one evening reading aloud from a recent submission.

"She's also writing under a pseudonym. I think I've started a trend," I said.

Quentin stroked his chin as thoughts flew in and out of his mind, like they entered through a revolving door. I sat down on the bed and crossed my oiled legs, which shimmered in the darkened room.

"Your pieces have been good. We've gotten good feedback. I'm sure you have fans," he said.

My journalistic hunger felt insatiable some days, but with Quentin's guidance we only published the best stories. My eyes scanned the submission ferociously; I searched for anything we could eat. He shut his laptop without warning, and I looked up at him, anticipating his departure.

"Is it late?" I asked him.

"I should get going."

He packed up his things and I stood up and smiled a little, before I turned and grabbed an envelope that was pinned down beneath a coffee mug on my desk. As he put on his backpack and tightened the straps around his arms, he paused a little when he turned to see me smiling. I extended the envelope to him.

"What's this?"

"An early birthday present."

Quentin's lips curled into a smile before he ripped open the unexpected gift and pulled out a pair of tickets to a book talk.

"You've quoted him a few times in your articles and I saw that he was coming."

"The tickets were sold out the same day."

He looked up at me in disbelief and I shrugged a little. Quentin's eyes softened at the sight of me then, and he looked down at the tickets once more to see if he had been deceived moments earlier.

"I made a way."

I slid my hands into the pockets of my athletic shorts and shuffled toward the door. With little effort, Quentin scooped me up into his arms and rested his face in the nook between my shoulder and my neck. When I felt his lips caress me there, my body stiffened like I'd been struck by lightning. His hands moved down to my lower back, before he pulled away and smiled a little. The delicate moment we shared was short-lived as Quentin soon disappeared like I'd grown accustomed to him doing. I was left with my thoughts, and a heart that beat a little faster.

***

Quentin quickly grew to be a close friend. We could talk for hours on the phone about obscure topics and random things we had in common. He paid attention to small details, like the rose gold studs I loved and the oversized Baja hoodie I wore religiously.

He folded the hoodie one evening while I typed steadily on my laptop, attempting to meet a deadline for my Psychology class.

"What are you doing?" He laid the piece of clothing on top of my backpack before he plopped down onto his bed and tossed his basketball up into the air. The rhythmic tossing and catching kept him occupied while I shushed him with my hand and continued to type.

"Send!" I sat back in the chair and exhaled. "In the nick of time."

It was 11:59 p.m.

"What topic did you choose?"

I stepped over the mounds of books Quentin had piled throughout his small bedroom. Occasionally, he'd invite me over for editing, but tonight I came by to get away from campus. The end of the semester ushered in an insufferable haze of anxiety, and libraries were filled to the brim.

"Nigresence," I said.

He lived in a house with a few of his fraternity brothers, and despite his active engagement with the frat, there was no visible paraphernalia in this room. When I sat down on the bed next to him and folded my legs, Quentin's face stirred, revealing a familiar look of amusement. I amused him, and I couldn't tell if it was because he found me witty or for a lesser reason – one that I didn't want to accept.

"Why?" he asked, as he flashed his wide smile.

"There's no story here," I shrugged. "Stop laughing at me. I haven't even said anything."

"I like your stories." His beam softened, as he lied back and looked over at me. "Why'd you pick a black racial identity model, Nia?" He chuckled.

"Because there weren't any that were discussed the entire semester."

His cackle filled the room and I lied down next to him, allowing a small giggle to escape my lips. He and I shared the view of the ceiling together before I turned my head toward him. My feelings for him were not platonic, but I'd grown comfortable in the friend zone. He made my chest feel warm and tight, but not like a panic attack – something sweeter.

"What does your tattoo mean?" I asked.

The house was still. His fraternity brothers were gone and the world outside only hummed and buzzed with a whisper. My words seemed to bounce off of the walls while I waited for him to respond. He flipped over his wrist, revealing the cryptic tattoo I'd noticed months ago. Each time I caught a glimpse of it, I wanted to ask, but the timing never felt right.

"If you look closer, you can still see the scar."

I slid closer to him and propped myself up on my elbow. I took his hand into mine before I ran my finger over the now apparent scar. His eyes traced my face as our breathing synchronized. "When did you..."

"When I was sixteen." He was quick to answer. Quick to tell me how he'd lost more than he knew he had – a best friend to gun violence, a father to prison, a grandmother to cancer. "I didn't think I'd grow up to be much of anything or anybody. It was a dark time."

My eyes welled as I imagined the depths from which he'd crawled. Quentin raised his hand and rested it on my cheek and his cool fingertips set me on fire. In the darkened room, I shut my eyes and imagined our skin merging into a beautiful smattering of brown. As Quentin sat up to kiss me, I placed my hand on his chest and jerked my head back. I'd dreamt of this moment for weeks! But here I was, terrified of the *dark* and how vast it suddenly felt.

"I'm sorry, did I do something wrong?" His voice was riddled with regret.

"No, it's me," I said softly. "I should go."

CHAPTER 6.

The best part of being a journalist was the uniform. It was what we wore – how we carried ourselves into the work we did. A few times, Quentin allowed me to tag along while he did interviews for potential stories. Quentin's *uniform* was impartiality. That's what he wore, and it manifested as a stoic expression with eyes that focused more on what he wrote than on the subject.

He often critiqued me when he would come to my interviews, stating that I was too invested in the subject and not invested enough in the story. He and I argued this point often, for I believed that the subject was the story.

When an email came through to my personal address for Brown Girl, I initially planned to share it with Quentin. But after seventy-two hours of mulling over the contents of the message, I decided to follow up on my own. I struggled with what I should *wear* to this interview, so I showed up bare.

I was resistant to use recording applications on my cell phone, so I carried a small recorder. When I pulled it out at the interview with this student, her glossy eyes crawled all over it.

"Is it okay for me to record our conversation?" I asked.

The student sat in front of me with eyes that looked like glass. She wore a dark hoodie that cast a shadow on her neck, but when she pulled the hood back, a head full of loose curls and puffy eyelids were revealed. Beneath her pain, there were beautiful cheekbones that attempted to emerge when she forced a smile.

"The recorder is fine. I figured you'd need one anyway."

I opened up my notebook to a fresh page and looked over at her. She pulled the sleeves of the hoodie up, revealing lines across her wrists that were darker than the rest of her arm.

"I call these my battle scars," she whispered. "He grabbed me here. They haven't completed healed."

"What has healed?" I asked.

She smiled a little, shoving the sleeves back down and sending me a hollow glance.

"Nothing."

"Would you tell me about that night? I have the email, but I want your story to be told the way that you envisioned."

She looked over her shoulder, like she was searching for an ever-present threat that could be lurking around the bookshelves we hid between in the abandoned library. She and I decided to meet after peak hours, to have some quiet. After a few moments of pause, Alicia seemed more comfortable. She sank in her seat and studied the worn wooden table we shared.

"I went to a party with some of the girls on my floor. I'm one of few black girls, but I've made some friends. My roommate was invited to a party at a fraternity house, so we went. The guy who answered the door seemed to be reluctant to invite me in – the party was basically all white."

I scribbled nearly incoherent notes while she spoke. I spent more time studying her and making a mental note of the beautiful human in front of me.

"I started drinking, and there was this guy there. I assumed he was part of the frat because he kept going in and out of these bedrooms with other guys at the party. As I was drinking, he would kind of come up and say little jokes. I'm not really interested in white guys, but I played along. After I had more than enough drinks, I told my roommate that I was ready to go. When she said that she didn't want to, I started to head back to the dorm on my own when the guy from earlier stopped me. He offered another drink and I obliged to be nice."

"Why?" I interjected, as my eyebrows lifted with curiosity.

"Part of me thinks that he would've gotten aggressive if I said no. Another part of me realizes that it doesn't really matter now. Whatever happened next is foggy still, but I know I stumbled home that night and found blood in my underwear and my wrists were black and blue."

"Did you call the police when you got back to the dorm?" I asked.

"I did, and I ended up going to the hospital. They did an exam, and I answered a bunch of questions. I've followed up with the precinct probably twelve times now. They always tell me that there is someone working on my case but I know how this all works."

"So why'd you write to me?" I asked.

Alicia looked over at me, and tears grew at the pits of her eyes. Her lips were shut tight, like she was fighting to keep the words in. She shook her head in despair and shrugged her shoulders – but they barely lifted because she was carrying so much.

"You were probably the only person who would care. I read your articles in *By Any Means* all of the time and if this story was ever going to be told, I wanted it to be by you," she said.

"How do you feel now?"

"Ripe…and raw. Like somebody reached in and stole my seeds, toyed with them with their tongue before they spit them back onto me; like I ain't got seeds anymore."

My eyes flooded and I was unafraid to let the tears fall. Impartiality be damned, for I knew the length and width of this type of pain. I'd committed the shape of it to memory. I was Alicia.

***

With a solemn jerk of the head, Quentin tossed the story onto my lap before he wiped his hand over his face. Alicia and I spoke a few more times before I wrote the story's first draft. With her permission, I pitched it to Quentin to be published in *By Any Means*. He stood up and shoved his hands into his pockets before he walked mechanically around his small bedroom. A deep sigh from the gut left Quentin's lips before he shook his head – a fervent *no*.

"This isn't our story."

"This isn't *our* story? A black girl got raped at a white fraternity house on this campus, and law enforcement isn't doing anything about it. How is this not *our* story, Quentin?"

"It just isn't, Nia. You can't see the forest for all of the trees. Your emotional investment in this story is laudable, but there's no place for it in this magazine."

I sat still and quiet on his bed as my eyes traversed the outline of a man I thought I knew. He sat down on the bed next to me and took my hands into his, before he put his face close enough to mine that I could smell the delicate mix of the day's sweat and his signature scent.

"Our magazine can't afford to go down this road. We'd open the floodgates for rape cases across this campus. It's not a race issue."

"She's *black*," I reiterated. Veins had to be popping out of my neck because my throat was on fire. "We care about the narratives of people who look like us. We provide a platform for people too often silenced by a society that could give a shit about what we go through. How does our rejection of this story perpetuate that same silencing?"

"I'm not silencing *her*, but I am deading this story. At least for us."

I stood up and shoved the story in my bag while Quentin watched. He leant back on his arms, before he cocked his head to the side and rolled his eyes out of frustration.

"Maybe you should stop cherry picking Audre Lorde quotes," I mumbled.

"Come again?" He leant forward with a smile of satisfaction on his face. He'd hit a button and I'd continue to engage him in this conversation – two things he enjoyed.

"Intersections of identities – to be both black and a woman – cannot be ignored. How convenient that you've chosen to do so. If you really understood what you read, you'd know that Lorde advocates for those of us on the margins *and* at the intersections."

"You're right."

I swung my bag over my shoulder and tossed him a look before I headed toward the door with little left to say. "I'm sorry if this upsets you, Nia."

He had no idea how much this "upset" me. I let the door slam behind me before I jogged down the steps with a fiery determination to tell Alicia's story.

***

"Girl if you don't sit down."

"I'm anxious to see it." I said.

Cecilia was on her computer at the desk in my dorm room, while I paced the floor, biting my nails and waiting for her to finish the task. Cici was majoring in Computer Science, and she created websites on the side for money. When I went to her with puppy-dog eyes and an endearing story, she offered her service for free.

"What do you think of the URL? Is it…catchy? Memorable?"

"Nia Marie Landrey, shut up. It's perfect. Leave me be."

I plopped down on my bed with a thud before Cecilia leaned back with a self-assured smirk. She cracked her fingers and spun around in the desk chair. "Voila!"

I stood up and walked to the computer. She'd built a website for *Brown Girl*, and I scrolled through the vacant webpages with a slack-jawed mouth. I shook my head and smiled. "Oh Cici. This exceeds my expectations."

She showed me how to update pages and stuck around while I published my first story – Alicia's story. Cecilia looked down at her hands while I read the story aloud. My throat coated with tears. I turned and looked at Cecilia to find her face full of emotion before she allowed her lips to rise. A small smile emerged. "You're doing the right thing."

"Let's do it," I mumbled.

I turned back around and Cecilia stood up and leant over behind me. "Do you have the subscription list for *By Any Means* in the Excel document?"

"Check."

Cecilia replaced me in the chair and with a few keystrokes, an email blast was sent to all of the subscribers of Quentin's magazine. I bit my lip and looked over at my phone. I anticipated an angry phone call. Cecilia looked up at me. "Were you really that surprised?" she asked.

"Surprised about what?"

"Quentin's decision not to publish this."

"I was," I nodded.

Although I had no reason to be. Like the men before him, Quentin proved to be a disappointment. Late nights spent together in my dorm and a mutual love of blackness brought me to believe that I knew him. The startling realization that I didn't left me shook. But more than that, I realized that Quentin didn't know me. For the first time in our friendship, I hadn't felt *seen* by him.

As the night grew long, I lied in bed and listened to my phone chime. I didn't bother to turn it off, for the chimes filled the space in a way that I couldn't. I was proud of myself. Damn proud. But part of me still yearned for his validation and that kept me up that night. *Why did his approval matter so much*? I rolled over and stared into the darkness as my phone lit up the ceiling, projecting a hollow white light.

CHAPTER 7.

I thought I knew him. He and I grew up together.

I had too much to drink, but I trusted him.

All I could think was – how could I be so irresponsible?

Transcribing had gotten easier with time. Two-hour interviews could take me an entire week to transcribe, but the work was meaningful. Whenever I could find a quiet spot – the library, my residence hall's lobby, empty classrooms on Saturdays – I typed until my hands went numb. These stories became my own and I vowed to tell them – to yell them from the treetops, with the same courage it took these women to come forward.

We were strangers before, but as their words left their lips, we became sisters. We were sisters who understood that the female body – the *black* female body – was often under threat. And beyond the body, we knew that psychological trauma was the scar that we couldn't cover. Hell, half of the time there wasn't foundation that was dark enough.

"Alicia's Story" sparked a campus-wide conversation on rape culture, and for the first time on Monroe's campus, a white woman wasn't at the center. *Brown Girl* received thousands of hits each month, but I was still draped in a cloak of anonymity until I felt brave enough to come forward. I began to feel like a coward; I was asking women to be their full selves, to take off the heaviest parts of their pain and allow me to carry the burden with them. Even with a request this big, I wasn't prepared to do the same. Not yet.

Since the platform's success, Cecilia hadn't returned any of my messages. When I stopped by her dorm to see her, she sent her roommate to the door to shoo me away. My persistence grew out of a desire to fix whatever I'd done. Cecilia was by far the best friend I had on this campus. One evening, she showed up at my door with a peace offering: some cookies and the *Living Single* box set. We got comfortable on my makeshift sofa, and I didn't ask her about where she'd been, or why today was any different.

She and I laughed until our stomachs were full of knots. Eventually the cookies were gone, but our hunger wasn't. We paused the show and started the trek to College Avenue for food. The quiet that settled in, outside of cookies and witty nineties platitudes, drove Cecilia to tears. When I stopped in the middle of the sidewalk to console her, the reason for her absence spilled onto the concrete. "The stories...the assaults were too familiar. They felt so familiar and I needed time to process. I'm sorry that I went ghost on you."

Cecilia's admission confirmed what I thought I knew.

"It's okay. I'm just glad that you've finally come around. Have you ever told anyone about it?"

She chuckled. "No." The two of us began to walk again. This time, the pace was slower while she got her thoughts together. "I couldn't tell anyone. I was too ashamed."

"Ashamed of what?" I asked.

"Ashamed of all of it...but mostly my own weakness. How could I allow someone to take advantage of my body?"

"*Allow?*"

"I should've fought back." She stopped again, and when her tears began to fall onto the collar of her jacket, she didn't bother to wipe them away. "But part of me felt like, if I fight, I might not make it out of here."

"Who was he?" My voice was only a hint above a whisper. We were standing close to each other as students around us headed to the bars with reckless abandon. Cecilia's eyes fell to the ground before she turned and continued to walk. She shoved her hands into her pockets and sniffled a little before she craned her neck to see me glued to the sidewalk.

"He doesn't deserve a name," she said.

I caught up with her and the two of us walked side by side in silence before Cecilia's lips parted.

"...I'm still wondering when you'll tell me about your assault."

"I haven't told anyone," I said.

"Well now you have."

***

Since I started this work, the stories haunted me. The fear and the fights drifted in and out of view with bold and striking clarity. Cecilia's story kept me up like the others. Only worse, because I loved her and her pain immediately became my own.

Since she opened up, I considered coming forward as the woman behind the computer, but the potential for backlash was loud enough to silence my bravery. *Brown Girl* was very different from Nia. Nia was afraid. Nia was troubled by the stories she told. *Brown* Girl spoke truth, while Nia was haunted by her own.

When *Brown Girl* received an email to join a panel for women hosted by the Multicultural Center, I figured it might be time to step up.

"You should really do the panel, Nia." Cecilia bit the tip of her pen, and looked across the room at me while I attempted to complete a peer review for our English class. A jazz melody collided with a hip-hop beat and fought for dominance between our abandoned headphones. Her phone chimed before she popped her gum. The various sounds caused me to slam the laptop shut and lie back on the bed.

"I can't focus," I said.

"Your conscience is eating away at you," she said.

Cecilia was staying with me temporarily. She and her roommate were having issues, and the water in her dorm was shut off twice this semester. When she asked if she could sleep on my "sofa," I welcomed the company.

"The stakes feel higher with my own work. I'm nervous."

"Nervous about what?" Cecilia asked. She sat up and chuckled. "You're acting like you didn't sign up for this when you stole that listserv and sent it off."

"I'm sensitive about my shit,"

"You ain't Badu, but you are Nia. And Nia is fearless – even in her cowardice. Rub on some coconut oil and burn some sage before you go to the panel."

"I don't think I can smudge an entire campus."

"Look, I opened up to you because you made me feel like I could. *Brown Girl* gives black women the space to connect to the part of themselves that we often neglect. When we talk about black girl magic, I think we focus too much on the lighter side of our existence. But the real black girl magic, the part that *Brown Girl* brings out, lives in the shadows. I mean look at me? A manifestation of both – light and dark."

She accented her speech with a smile, and I allowed the words to hang in the room before I sat up and looked over at her. She and I locked into each other's gaze and stayed there.

"I'll do the panel. Under one condition though – you have to let me write your story."

Cecilia shrugged. "Only after you write yours."

Nia's Story
Brown Girl

My daddy was bow-legged as a boy, and to my mother's chagrin, I took my first steps with crooked legs like him. He and I were more alike than she wanted to acknowledge, and despite our mismatched skin, I took on the shape of his nose, and his high cheekbones – the things my mother loved most about his face. In the mirror, I could trace the frame of his countenance with my own fingers, but the touch grew distant with time. The longer he was away, the more I resembled a stranger in my own mirror.

I hadn't seen my daddy in a month of Sundays, but I remembered the sound of his car horn. When I heard the rusted engine enter the driveway, I hopped off of my bed and scurried to the hall to see my mother walking to the door to meet him. These types of visits were the extent of our relationship. I knew at a young age that I couldn't count on him to show up if it wasn't on his time. My father, in his half-grown manhood and microwaved affection attempted to love she and I with less than a heart before he gave up all together.

A long, dainty girl with skin like honey climbed out of the car and my mother's breath hitched in her throat at the sight of her. Few things were different about my daddy, but his hair had peppered over and his lanky stroll had become a pitter-patter with age. I can't remember much about that day. When he revealed that the dainty girl was my sister, there was an indiscernible explosion in my body and my hands went cold.

Weeks later, I complained of a headache, and my mother attempted to remedy the cloudiness with head rubs and lonely "I love you's." I prayed for transparency and emotional nudity, but grew closed and morose instead. My mother moved like water – washed over with delicacy – but my father settled at the bottom of me like sediment. His heaviness cemented me, and I stayed tethered to him. I settled in obdurateness. I hardened by choice.

I didn't see my sister, even when my mother tried to foster a relationship between the two of us. Explanations from my father were not accepted, phone calls were ignored, and letters were returned to sender. He was a dead-end, a stutter-step that disappeared into the distance. The headaches didn't subside, and each day I woke to the feeling of tiny hammers and fists pounding away at my cranium. Much like my heart, my head hadn't grown accustomed to the pain. The headaches stopped soon after I cut my hair. Cutting with those shears was the closest I could get to the pain.

I scrubbed away every ounce of my father, and any semblance felt like a betrayal to myself. No longer bow-legged, I stood on legs that afforded me the strength to walk away from who he was. Unknowingly, I walked into another set of arms, and much to my demise, his resembled my daddy's.

When times were good, my body would flood with butterflies and fireflies, all tangled up together in my stomach. I was never a daddy's girl, but this guy made me feel like I was somebody's girl. He cradled my heart in his hands before he watched it detonate like a crimson grenade. Part of me disappeared one night in his bedroom when I discovered that rage and love could be mistaken for one another. That virginity was a virtue when its absence meant you were left with scars – literal and figurative.

I didn't know much about life or love or longing at the time, but I knew that my tears signified brokenness. I cracked. When the tears didn't stop for months, I knew that it was because of the two of them. Tears had the strength to destroy, to drown. Tears could strangle the life out of you – leave you breathless, without words. They were outward manifestations of inward pain and seeing them meant that I had to reckon with that pain; that I had to acknowledge that it was there.

I no longer cry for them – both of them are gone, now. But there will always be shame and a persistent battle between reverence and resentment. I reserved a seat for them for too long. I counted cars on Saturdays, hoping theirs would be next. I danced with their silhouettes on my tippy toes. I checked the mail for apologies.

I made a home out of memories, and I set the table – waiting for them, for too long.

The pen is powerful – powerful enough to write yourself out of your own story. No longer will I be invisible in light of their mistakes. Consider this absolution.

CHAPTER 8.

For months after I was raped, I existed outside of my body. He'd murdered some part of me. Pried me open like a pomegranate, allowed the blood of my fruit to stain his fingers. I didn't have a say in any of it. I didn't say anything at all.

It happened on a Thursday. He shared a cramped two-bedroom apartment with his father a few blocks from our school. The apartment was never clean, nor warm. The chill rattled my bones while he tidied the small space, hoping to make me feel comfortable.

Let's go to my room.

I could remember his breath flooding my nostrils and the weight of his frame pressed against mine. His calloused hands moved around my body like a fool stumbling in the dark, and I hadn't felt pleasure in that moment, just fear.

"Well let's slow down. I'm not ready."

Don't you love me?

There was a slap across the face, before my wrists were pressed into the bed he'd sleep in every night after the rape.

For months, I survived by existing outside of my body like I did that night. Watching my person – watching *me* – be scavenged and left to die. Surely, he'd murdered some part of me.

***

I fought for my life through my words – an admirable act, but one that didn't always feel substantial.

I agreed to sit on the panel for the Multicultural Center, and I cowered next to the women I shared the stage with. These were women who'd *actually* done something, like AIDS research or photojournalism projects on gentrification. When it was time for my biography to be read, I sat up and smiled, staring out at the indiscernible faces in the crowd. Part of me was grateful for the darkened audience. I couldn't see anyone and I found some comfort in that.

To my surprise, applause erupted from the room when the moderator revealed that I was the woman behind *Brown Girl*. My chest rose and I sat up a little straighter then. *You're somebody,* I thought.

I was asked the first question: *Why did you start a publication like Brown Girl?* I pulled the microphone around to me and stared out at the seemingly endless audience.

"As many of you know, I have written for another publication here at Monroe, and it was a great experience. It gave me a lot of insight into publishing, things that I simply wasn't aware of. It drove me to really define my audience and my voice. With time, I grew to discover that there really wasn't a space for *me*. In my entirety, my blackness and womanness could not truly be explored or expressed in that space. So I started my own publication."

"Could you tell us more about your experience with *By Any Means?*" the moderator asked.

I couldn't see anyone in the audience and I was relying on that, until I could make out the shape of a familiar person standing in the back of the room. My brain, without my consent, filled in the shape of him and I knew immediately that it was Quentin.

"When I first came to Monroe, I wanted to be a black writer. I wanted to document, and I wanted to resist with my words. I thought that this was enough until I discovered that it wasn't. When I say that I'm a black woman, I struggle to decide which of those identities is operative. Which is most important? I shouldn't have to write for a publication for women and *By Any Means* to capture my voice. No, I'm going to write at the intersection because that's where I live. That's where I am – that's *who* I am. Those are the stories that I tell now – stories for and by women of color."

When the panel concluded, the lights came up and I scanned the room looking for a familiar face – for *Quentin*. Cecilia came to the stage beaming from ear to ear as I stepped down and walked to her.

"Thanks for being my wings on days when I'm too afraid to fly," I said to her.

"That's what we do, sis," she said. "How does it feel?"

"I feel relieved."

The crowd hung around after the panel. Women came forward with personal anecdotes; the stories I wrote resonated with so many of them on a visceral level. I listened and I cried – this is what I'd hoped for. I internalized the feedback, the goodness, the magic. I connected with women, set up coffee dates and made promises that I'd continue to tell stories until I couldn't.

As the room emptied and I gathered my things to leave, a smell I'd grown to love filtered into my nose and I turned around to see Quentin there with his hands resting in his pockets.

"Congrats on your success," he said softly.

"Thanks."

I put my bag on my shoulder and shrugged, "Couldn't have done this without your support. Thanks for giving me a shot."

"You would've gotten here without me." He smiled.

"I try to give credit where it's due."

"We can chat later about you stealing my listserv. No sweat, though."

I smiled and looked around the empty room. Quentin took his hands out of his pockets and stepped a little closer to me. He placed a hand on my arm, and our eyes tripped over each other's like they'd done so many times before.

"I wish you'd told me about what happened to you. The night I rejected Alicia's story, I stayed up for a while after you left wondering if I'd done the right thing. I can't say now that I have any resolve on the matter, but I know that I was too dismissive that night. And then you published your story and…it all made sense. I'm sorry, Nia."

I smiled to keep from crying in front of him. He noticed the tears growing in my eyes and pulled me into a hug before they fell. He ran his hands up and down my back, and my body relaxed into his. He left a small kiss on my cheek and I let go of the tears I'd been holding.

"You said I'd crack eventually," I whispered.

He sighed and tightened his embrace. "…But you aren't broken."

The lights in the room went off. It was late and the student union was closing. But he and I stood there with our arms wrapped around each other. For weeks, we'd been a world apart, but tonight the distance felt infinitesimal.

***

I've always admired my mother's hands. As a child, I'd challenge her, palm-to-palm, noting how fast my fingers were growing. *Soon they'd be longer than hers,* I used to say.

Her hands healed me for years. She tended to my scars after a fall on the playground or when I had an accident at basketball practice. A swipe across the forehead could assuage a headache; a warm caress on my cheek halted pain. When she read the story I'd published on *Brown Girl,* she came to a startling realization – there were parts of me that she couldn't touch.

Compounded with nine months of distance, my mother wasn't sure she knew the child sitting in front of her. I was the outline of the person she'd birthed, but this girl – this *woman* – colored herself in with her own crayon.

I pulled at my shorts, hoping they weren't riding up as I sat in front of my mother. Spring semester was nearly over, and she'd flown to Rhode Island to help me move out of my dorm. She sipped her glass of wine while I took gulps of the ice water I'd settled for.

"You're quiet," I said to her finally.

My mother's shoulders rose and fell as she cried in front of me. Maybe it was my tone, or the fact that I'd finished my first year of college. I wasn't sure. Startled, I raised my eyebrows and looked around the restaurant. "Ma?" I placed my hand over hers.

"You didn't tell me," she managed to say.

"I didn't tell anybody."

"Except you did," she said, as she dabbed her eyes and looked over at me. For the first time, I felt like I'd betrayed my mother. Like I'd built a secret alliance with a world she wasn't part of. "You told the world something you couldn't tell your mother."

I sank in my seat. "It was easier that way – to just write it and publish it."

"*...Was it Malcolm?*" she asked. Her voice trembled over his name.

I nodded my head and she looked down at her hands – her beautiful, useless hands. "I'll make arrangements with my therapist. You'll see her this summer."

"I don't want therapy," I refused.

"You need to talk to somebody, Nia. You've had this pent up for too long."

"I feel the most free I've felt since it happened, Ma. I don't need therapy. I just want to write." I smiled a little and put my hand over hers. "That's all I want – to write."

My mother's eyes traced the outline of the woman in front of her, but she smiled this time.

"Your hair looks good, Sweet Pea. It's grown out a lot."

PART II.
Twenty-Two

CHAPTER 9.

When my hair started to shed, I knew why.

I stood beneath the showerhead submerged in water. I could taste the salt of my tears as I pulled clumps of hair from the back of my head. I pressed each lost strand to the wall in memoriam. I'd tried finger detangling, denman brushes, and pre-shampoo routines. Hell, I'd even spent twenty dollars on a useless protein treatment. None of it worked.

"Did it shed any less this time?" Cecilia asked from her bedroom.

I shook my head as I adjusted my towel and turned off the bathroom light. I went into my room and started to shut the door when her hand stopped it from closing.

"Did you do what I told you? I think it's dry," she said. "Maybe your protein-moisture balance is off."

"I've done a bunch of hot oil treatments. I think I'm going to get a trim." I navigated the bedroom, walking around piles of books and clothes I hadn't put away. Cecilia followed, taking the same path before she stopped and stood in the middle of the floor.

I'd welcomed the sun this morning but it was gone already. The fall was here again. Cecilia and I were like shadows in my darkened room; a small lamp on my nightstand provided just enough light for us to avoid the piles of things I'd failed to put away. A messy room was common for me now.

"No, don't cut it," she said with a sigh. The space between her eyebrows wrinkled like an accordion. Her mind was in "problem solve" mode as she scanned the hair products on my dresser. I went into my closet and threw on some underwear and one of *his* t-shirts without noticing.

When I walked out of the closet, Cecilia's eyes fell to the shirt and her lips turned down into a small frown.

"Have you spoken to him?" she asked.

I looked down at the shirt before my gaze crawled up to hers. Her face softened with concern while I shrugged my heavy shoulders.

"We're done. I told you," I said.

"Seems to me like you two still have a lot to work out." She sat down on the bed and I shook my head vehemently. I didn't want to do this today.

I hadn't cried in seventy-two hours; hadn't drawn and re-drawn the shape of Quentin's face, or pictured the sullen hue he'd taken on the night we broke up. I didn't want to do any of that tonight.

The apartment that Cecilia and I now shared grew quiet. We moved into the apartment at the start of our junior year. It felt like home most days, but since the breakup, it was hard to be here. It was hard to be at Monroe. Everything reminded me of Quentin.

Cecilia studied me and pulled apart the discomfort I wore on my face. I pulled my knees in to my chest and wrapped my arms around them.

"I don't want to talk about it Cici," I whispered.

"I'll do some research," she blurted. Her scattered thinking was usually annoying and difficult to follow but tonight I welcomed the shift.

I raised an eyebrow. "Research on what?"

"Your hair breakage girl. I've already collected some samples." She stood up to leave and I smiled a little. The first time in days.

***

I hadn't gone to the hospital yet. Jacob's mother called, left a voicemail and sent a text. Her calls went unanswered for days and I carried the weight of my silence in my stomach like gallstones. This shit was painful.

Our sociology class was raising money for hospital bills – an unexpected expense for Jacob's family so close to the holidays. The course instructor, Nicholas, stood at the front of the room and completed the day's attendance. When he got to Jacob's name, he looked up at the empty seat and stammered a little. The abrupt pause sent a chill of unease through the classroom and the empty seat behind me suddenly felt closer than before.

When we started the class discussion, I didn't offer much. Jacob and I were usually the most talkative. We always argued in class – an indication of our many differences. Our disagreements were fueled by a stubborn commitment to our beliefs. We hadn't ever grown close, much to his mother's disappointment, but we'd developed a fair level of respect for each other. He wasn't an enemy but he wasn't a friend either. We shared interests in race and politics so we often selected the same classes. Despite my usual disdain for Jacob, I like to think that we made each other better, like iron sharpening iron. Our sparring matches in class were practice for the work I'd have to do as a journalist. I defended what I could; I stood my ground even when my adversary was black. While Jacob worked hard to distance himself from blackness, I drew closer. That was our biggest difference and it was the most difficult for us to overcome.

It wasn't surprising to find Jacob in my sociology class fall semester of our senior year. In this class, Nicholas encouraged our quarrels, finding them both amusing and engaging.

"You both are scholars. It's refreshing to watch you grapple with these topics. To be so different – literally on opposite ends of the philosophical and political spectrums – but so similar in your willingness to argue," he said once.

This was after another heated debate in class. The topic was police brutality and a smug Jacob managed to make light of a recent case in Providence. An unarmed nineteen-year-old black male was shot a few hundred feet from his home when a call was made about suspicious activity in his suburban neighborhood.

"If you aren't guilty, why are you running from the police?" he'd said. Emboldened by a few head nods from white students, he continued. "I'm not justifying undue force, but when an officer tells you to stop, follow the directions."

I turned around and looked up at him. "When was the last time you were stopped by the cops, Jacob?"

He smirked. "I haven't ever been stopped."

I nodded. My frown deepened.

"I pray that you never have an encounter with a cop but in the likely event that you do, I hope that you understand that the decision to run is a matter of fear and not guilt."

He and I met eyes and he kept his comments to himself for the rest of the discussion. After, he apologized for his callousness but remained unmoved in his stance on the topic.

Without him, class hadn't been the same. I wasn't the same either. After our fourth class without Jacob, I stood up and waited for most of the students to leave before I approached Nicholas at his desk. He was packing up his satchel when I cleared my throat. He looked up at me, smiled and put his bag on his shoulder.

"Walk with me."

I tightened the straps on my backpack and walked with him across the quad to his office in the sociology building. He rambled about a podcast he'd listened to, and I tried to listen – tried to clear my muddied thoughts.

We walked into the office and he turned on the lamp near the window. The blinds were closed and I could smell cinnamon from the apple cider in the staff lounge next door. I put my bag down in one of the chairs as Nicholas began to charge his laptop. He put on John Coltrane's "A Love Supreme" and pivoted toward the bookshelf.

"Tea?" he asked.

I nodded and watched him from the other side of the office. Nicholas was pursuing a doctorate in sociology. He and I connected last year when he was a teaching assistant for my social stratification course. When I saw his name listed as the instructor for this course – Race, Class and Gender – I signed up immediately.

He went down the hall to get some hot water for me and I stood up and studied the photos on his bookshelf – a dog, a woman that looked like his mom, a shot of the George Washington Bridge. His cologne preceded him as he returned. His plaid shirt hugged his broad shoulders and his muscles flexed when he extended his arm to hand me the mug of tea.

We settled in. I took slow, long sips as the sound of Coltrane's horn glided into my ears with warmth, like the tea going down my throat.

Nicholas ran his hand over his head before he looked toward his laptop. He'd recently gotten a line-up and it was razor sharp, like his striking jawline. I noted all of these things as we allowed the quiet to blanket the office.

"I'm surprised you spoke in class today," he said softly.

"That girl was being homophobic again. I had to call her out," I mumbled. My mouth was lost somewhere in the oversized scarf I wore.

"And then this happened..." he said.

I looked up as he turned his laptop toward me. I'd gotten a C- on my midterm. I sighed and dropped my head. "Dammit, Nick."

"I was disappointed," he said softly. "But more concerned. You haven't been the same since..." His voice trailed off.

A loaded pause.

"I can handle it. I'm managing it just fine."

"This isn't just fine Nia," he stated, with concern sewn into his brow.

"I was tired when I wrote it. I should've spent more time developing my ideas. It won't happen again, I promise." I turned away in shame and pulled out my computer. Nick rolled his chair closer to me and narrowed his eyes. I tossed him a crooked smile – an attempt to convince him that I was indeed *fine*.

"You know you can talk to me, right?" he asked. "Jacob means a lot to me too."

"I'm going through a breakup," I blurted.

I didn't want to talk about Quentin or the breakup either, but I'd do anything to keep my mind off of Jacob. I didn't want to remember the black and blue bruising on his face, or his lifeless, limp body being dragged away from the porch we shared moments earlier.

"I feel so sluggish. Like most days I wake up feeling like the world's foot is on my damn chest. It's hard to breathe, Nick. Like the rising and falling of my chest is an entire production now. I gotta *act* like I'm breathing," I said.

"You're supposed to start with your breath. Once you get that under control, the rest will fall into place," he said, sitting his cup down. "Sit up straight, like this."

He rested his back against the chair and placed his hands on his knees. I did the same and waited for him to speak.

"Your breath is too shallow. Breathe from the gut."

I did as he instructed, until I felt a light tingle dance up my legs to my chest. My lungs expanded until they were full like balloons. A loud breath escaped through my mouth and when I opened my eyes, I made out the shape of Nicholas in front of me. He leant forward.

"How long have you held your breath?" he asked.

"Too long I guess."

***

My hands trembled as I gathered another ball of lost hair from the floor. The collections had gotten bigger. I let out an audible sigh and my eyes watered at the sight of what I'd lost – another *mourning*. I tossed the hair in the trash before I went back to my laptop.

Just write Nia.

The cursor blinked at the top of a blank page. There were hundreds of words fighting to get out, maybe thousands, but I kept drawing blanks. I couldn't finish a sentence, couldn't articulate a thought. The words tripped over themselves, ideas collided until they were useless. I had writer's block – and I'd barely uttered a word since the night of the party.

My phone rang but I sat paralyzed by the blinking cursor, the frustration and the cruel, familiar tightening of my chest. I stared at that damn screen until my heavy eyelids fell.

An hour went by – nothing, still.

I had four missed calls. One from my mom, one from Cecilia and the other two from an unsaved number but one I recognized – Jacob's mother. I swallowed the rock in my throat and listened to the voicemail she'd left.

"Nia, it's Jacob's mom again. He's asking for you, sweetie."

The message ended. I searched the phone, hoping for more. There had to be more. Was there nothing else? He's asking for *me*?

I listened to the message at least a dozen times before I stood up and threw on some clothes – anything I could grab. When I appeared in the living room, Cecilia's mouth fell open with a cackle.

"Nia, where are you going dressed like that?"

My weak hand gripped the doorknob with uncertainty as I turned toward her and shut my eyes. "I'm going to see Jacob." The phrase felt offensive as it left my lips.

Cecilia's face fell a little, but she scrambled to pick it up, hoping to be brave for me. "Need me to go?"

"No. I have to do this on my own."

***

The stale smell of the hospital caused my stomach to turn when I arrived. I feverishly searched the walls for room 358. The halls were all a blinding white and I couldn't distinguish one turn from another. When I finally found the recovery ward, I stopped in front of Jacob's room and looked down at my empty hands.

I should've brought something, I thought.

I could hear his mother's voice over the faint sound of the television. I knocked softly, took a few deep breaths, and pushed the door open. Jacob's mother Angela stood up and smiled. "Ms. Nia. It's good to see you."

I fell into her embrace and apologized for the delay. She rubbed my back and assuaged my shame. She refused to accept my apologies. I couldn't bear to look at him yet, but Jacob sat up slowly on the bed and waited for me to turn toward him.

"I'll let you two talk," she said.

The door to the room closed and I stood with my back to him. Jacob was staring a hole through my head, the heat of his gaze causing my scalp to perspire.

"Nia," he said. His voice was low and breathy as he struggled to push out my name.

I dropped my head and allowed myself to burst open at the seams. Tears fled my eyes and my body shook. Jacob turned and grabbed one of his crutches off of the wall. When I heard movement behind me, I spun around to see him standing.

My breathing slowed and I took a few steps toward him. He offered a brave smile and I bit my lip to stop the loud cry that attempted to escape. "Jacob," I whispered, as I placed my hand on his cheek.

He was himself – beneath scars that weren't healing as quickly as I hoped. His top lip had been sewn back together with stitches. His beautiful cheekbones were forever altered, as one appeared to be deflated. My index finger traced the swollenness of his left eye before I placed a hand on his chest.

"I'm sorry it took so long."

He shook his head and offered an uneven smile once more, before he pointed at the chair next to the bed. "Sit, will you?"

"Of course," I said. I unwrapped my scarf and sat down in the chair that faced his bed. He resumed his spot and tried to get comfortable.

"Anything broken?" I asked.

I already knew. I'd read every article and watched all of the news coverage since the night of the party. He had a bruised lung and an eye socket fracture. His lip was split and there was some damage done to his left leg.

"I may have to have surgery on my eye but everything else is healing okay." His speech was slow and steady. He took a few shallow breaths between thoughts.

Before, I couldn't imagine looking at him. But now – now I couldn't take my eyes off of him. My heart swelled with sympathy.

"Your mom said that you wanted to see me," I said finally.

He nodded. "How's sociology?" he asked.

I rolled my eyes and smiled a little. "You wanted me to come tell you about class? Predictable. I don't think you're in the position to argue."

He smiled and shook his head. "Wanted something else."

"Anything," I said softly.

When Jacob took me out for ice cream years ago, he barely looked at me. But today, he traced my face with intention. Eye contact from Jacob was different – startling almost. He held the gaze with certainty before he parted his lips.

"…I want you to write about me again."

CHAPTER 10.

I started writing stories in middle school. Climbing up onto the couch in our sunroom, I'd scan the stack of discarded newspapers and search for stories that I found interest in. Stories of heroism, loss, and grief – I read them all and attempted to rewrite them. Out of my childish curiosity and endless imagination, I wrote stories that were based on the truth, but nestled comfortably under the guise of fiction.

Even now, I found refuge in storytelling. I had a small staff for *Brown Girl* – mostly journalism majors and student activists who wanted more than Twitter to express themselves. I was the editor in chief and Cecilia joined me as the creative director. We were publishing comfortably with five writers and I didn't see a need to expand any time soon. Despite our small size, we had a lot of opinions. An agenda that should take twenty minutes to move through could take us hours. We were young. We were passionate.

At Monday's meeting, Cecilia sat off in the corner like she always did. She half-listened but we all knew that she was doing homework or finishing up an assignment at the last minute. She and I shared a propensity for procrastination.

"I thought the piece on Rihanna's make-up collection had a lot of fluff," Nneka said as she pulled out another Now and Later. Her long, acrylic nails scraped the sides of the squared candy as she tried to pop the wrapper open. I watched her for a while before I snatched it from her and unwrapped it myself.

Priya pushed her silky black hair up into a ponytail and rolled her eyes before she shrugged. "And *you* haven't pitched anything worthy of publishing in like two months."

"Can we focus, please?" I interjected.

Maybe I should've taken my own advice. *I* couldn't focus. Since Jacob asked me to write his story, I thought about that and nothing else. But I hadn't written anything at all.

"…I've been asked to write about the night of the party," I said finally.

The room fell quiet and Cecilia shut her laptop then. I tapped my pen lightly on the edge of my laptop and studied my team.

"What do you guys think?" I asked.

"I think that's a story better suited for *By Any Means*," Nneka said. "Don't get me wrong, I think Jacob deserves to have his story told but this is supposed to be a publication for women of color."

"That's where I'm getting stuck too," I said softly. "But I don't have contacts at *BAM* that I trust anymore."

I needed to write this and I had to publish it. Jacob trusted *me* to be in charge of crafting the narrative he'd share with the world. I couldn't mess this up.

"I know Jacob means a lot to you so...do what you think is best. But I'm with Nneka. I don't want us to lose sight of our mission," Priya said.

When the girls left, I looked over at Cecilia while she packed up to leave. She walked toward me with her bag hanging from her shoulder.

"So what are you going to do Ms. Landrey?"

I shrugged and shook my head, "I don't know."

"Could you...call Quentin? Maybe see if he could talk to the editor at *BAM* and get Jacob's story published over there?"

"*BAM* isn't what it was when Quentin was here. Besides, he doesn't want to talk to me."

"You don't know that, Nia..."

"Just drop it, Cici. Quentin isn't an option."

She shrugged and nodded her head toward the door. "Well you can't write the story tonight. Let's make a stop on the way home and get your mind off of everything."

"Do we have to?" I asked. "I'm exhausted. I just want to sleep."

"Your first class isn't until eleven. You'll live."

***

As we crossed the quad, the wind tousled my dry, brittle curls. I pushed the neglected hair up into a puff and allowed Cecilia to lead the way. When we got to College Avenue, I knew exactly where we were headed. Tony's – Cici's favorite bar.

I scooted through tables with two glasses of wine in my hands. "Excuse me." I sounded like a broken record. There were black people everywhere seeking the same things: community, fellowship, belonging. Tony's was different from the other bars on Monroe's campus. On Thursdays, the DJ dared to play hip-hop and black students could enjoy themselves without pretense. It was a safe space to be black – one of the few spaces at Monroe.

I was on drink duty while Cici found a table for us. When I found her, she cradled her phone in her hands and waved me over. I smiled at her and pushed through the sea of bodies. I took off my jacket, leaving my mahogany skin draped in a thin white top. Her head was on a swivel as she scanned the room looking for familiar faces. She stopped her scan abruptly and slid down in her chair. I studied her over my wine glass.

"What is wrong with you?" I asked.

"He's here girl!"

My heart fell into my stomach.

Was Quentin here? Why would he be here?

"Who?" I asked as I turned and looked around the bar.

"Don't look, fool! The dude I went on that Tinder date with last week. He probably knew I'd be here. I told him this was my favorite spot."

When my heart rate returned to normal, I shook my head at her. "Well that was stupid. Guess we can't come here anymore." I shrugged.

"You have no reason to avoid this place. We'll be back! Cheers!"

She tapped my glass without me joining her. The music went on, with bass vibrating the table we shared. I tapped my feet against the floor and Cecilia danced in her seat. She shut her eyes and let the music consume her for a moment. We all did. We let go of our woes. We screamed Future lyrics at the top of our lungs and sang Drake hooks in unison like we were a choir.

The energy in the bar shifted when I heard the chimes over the door. I turned around to see who'd entered. Cecilia folded her arms and smacked her lips at the sight of them. "Why do they always show up on Thursdays?"

There were two of them standing guard at the door. One held his hand over his gun – a subtle threat, but one I didn't take lightly. The DJ turned down the music and a few students decided to leave. I took another sip of my wine, hoping to subdue the anxiety I suddenly felt. It clawed at my chest. The mere presence of cops made the walls sweat. We were young. We were afraid. We were black.

Another student and I locked eyes across the bar as she took a deep breath and clinched her fists with fear, *or fury*. Maybe both. I stood up and watched as she climbed onto the bar and thrust her fist into the air. "JUSTICE FOR JACOB!" she yelled.

The crowd cracked open and yelled back, fighting the tension in the bar. She called and they responded until her voice was hoarse. I stood up and put on my coat before I navigated the bar with misty eyes. Cecilia's voice faded as I walked outside into the cold December night. Jacob deserved to tell his story.

Too many just like him didn't have the opportunity.

Unlike them, he was alive.

***

I was back in front of the blank screen. I reached around to scratch the back of my head and my hair loosened without struggle, latching onto my fingernails. I studied the lost strands while my hands shook on the keyboard.

I needed to relax.

Quentin's smile appeared, dancing in front of me like a mirage on the screen of my laptop. He'd always been the antidote to my anxiety, and I thought back to a conversation we had months earlier.

"My pain isn't poetry, Quentin," I said to him.

"Your pain isn't poetry but it's purposeful. Write it down," he responded.

Your pain is purposeful, your pain has purpose.

I repeated this to myself before I allowed memories from the night of the party to crawl out of the box I'd put them in. The memories unfolded – they were bold, startling. I wrote down all that I could remember, even when it hurt.

***

I didn't want to go to the party, and I thought about this fact each morning since that night. Cecilia stood at my bedroom door pleading with me.

"I have a deadline at eleven. If I can finish my paper in time, I will join you," I said.

"You promise? Don't stay in the house talking to Quentin tonight."

"I promise, Cecilia. I'll text you if I can come."

So I did. I sent a short text before I got into the back of an uberPOOL and rode with three other students to campus. A few members of the Black Student Union's executive board had a house two blocks away from campus and they were hosting a homecoming party. I arrived with few expectations and little desire to stay longer than an hour.

As I approached, I scanned the massive party. The house crawled with students. A low, steady bass line shook the porch I stood on as I texted Cecilia and asked her to meet me outside. I found an empty spot on the banister and looked around for people I knew. Jacob's face came into view and I furrowed my brow, surprised to see him.

"What's that face?" he asked, as he approached me with a beer in his hand.

"You never come to black functions," I said.

"That's not true. Actually, *you* don't come to black functions anymore. Not since your precious Quentin graduated."

"I have a short list of things that I hate and you're on it," I said, looking up at him.

He smiled and shrugged before he sat down next to me. Red and blue lights suddenly lit up the front of the house and at once, our breathing synchronized – all three hundred of us, black and brown and bare.

Jacob stood up and finished off his beer as four cop cars approached the curb. Officers hopped out and hysteria ensued. Students were shoved without reason and racial epithets dangled from the cops' mouths like fangs. Another night ruined. I stood up and Jacob held me back with his arm as he watched the scene unfold in the front yard.

While most students left the party, a group of them remained in the front yard and refused to leave. Jaden, a student I'd known since my first year at Monroe, yelled at the cops. His slurred speech and unsteady stance, signs of his inebriation, only fueled the cops' agitation. Jacob and I watched from the porch until Jaden was thrown to the ground.

"Shit. I'll be back." Jacob tossed his beer can over the banister.

"Jacob, wait..."

He walked down the steps and onto the grass. "Jaden, you good?" Jacob emerged from the dark porch with his hands in his pockets – a deadly mistake.

"Jacob!" I yelled from the top of the steps, immediately recognizing the error.

Jacob turned when I called his name to find a gun pointed at him. A white, trembling finger hovered over the trigger. "Hands up!"

Students ran out of the house and jumped off of the porch. They ran toward the backyard, hopped over fences. Anything to get away from the gun.

The gun.

I trembled on the porch and watched Jacob raise his hands above his head. He pleaded with the officer, but the gun didn't move. Time slowed and I couldn't catch my breath – couldn't *feel* my breath. I tried to move toward him but my feet were still like they'd been bolted to the aged, wooden planks of the porch.

Another cop approached Jacob from behind and forcefully handcuffed him.

"What the fuck! I didn't do anything!"

Jacob struggled to free his hands as the sharp handcuffs cut into his wrists like knives. His large frame was difficult to manage by the female cop so she yelled for the others. I managed to drag my feet toward the steps. I gripped the railing and cried out but there were no words.

I'm sure that this was when the writer's block started.

With a struggle, Jacob was hit against the head with the butt of a gun and pushed to the ground, pent down with knees in his back. I covered my mouth as Jacob looked up at me through his bloodied eye – his face pressed against the pavement.

"Nia...Nia please call my mom. Please," he cried. Blood splattered from his lips and I watched as they dragged his limp body to the car. He'd stopped fighting, but it was far too late.

CHAPTER 11.

On August 9, 2014 a black boy in Ferguson, Missouri lied against the pavement in the summer sun. He was there for hours like a discarded orange peel tossed to rot. His name was Michael Brown. The news swept the nation and the desire to resist spread across college campuses like wildfire. The Black Student Union assembled immediately. *Brown Girl* and *By Any Means* were charged with covering campus protests and forums. We wore black in solidarity with protestors in Ferguson. We cried together. We prayed for his mother. We prayed for each other. We mourned, until malice met us where we'd least expected it – at Monroe.

Two months after Michael Brown's death, Jacob lied in a hospital bed breathing through a bruised lung, seeing through a fractured eye, speaking with damaged lips, and tending to a broken spirit. I had nightmares about them – all of them. Black bodies. Black boys. The thoughts were too much to bear. I felt like I was going crazy.

I called my mom for some comfort, some wisdom – for the warmth that only she could provide. Her eyes crawled all over me, looking for dents and scratches; for any sign of why I'd asked her to come to town. I licked my fingertips and turned the page of a book I was reading for my English class, before I grabbed my pen and scribbled a note in the margin. My mother let a deep sigh leave her lips before she looked out of the window.

"You haven't put that book down since I picked you up."

I folded the corner of the page I was reading and closed the book before I forced a smile and grabbed another pack of sugar for my tea. Books were an escape… and I was also behind in English.

"I'm sorry," I responded. "How was your flight?"

"Is that a book for one of your classes? Are you falling behind, Marie?"

The use of my middle name was never casual. It was always intentional. The name hung in the air and I sucked my teeth like a child.

"I'll be fine. I've basically slept through my classes this semester. It's been easy to manage."

I was lying. I was drowning in work and it was hard to keep up with *Brown Girl* lately. Most evenings, I found myself lying in bed at the end of the day, staring at the same spots on the walls.

"You've never been forthright while you're struggling. I honestly can't tell the truth from a lie anymore."

"What have I lied about, Ma?" I whined.

"What *haven't* you lied about?" She chuckled. "Somewhere between freshmen year and now, you shut our door of communication. I think it was when Quentin entered the picture."

I rolled my eyes. "I don't agree."

"When's the last time you called me just to catch up?" she asked.

"I'm busy, Ma."

"Well who do you talk to? About the breakup and... everything else?" she inquired.

"Ma, please."

She put her hand over mine and searched my face. "Nia...you have to stop bottling everything up. It'll kill you. You know that? Stress...it will kill you."

"I'm not stressed." I smiled and shook my head. Tight-lipped and uncomfortable, I shifted in my chair and folded my arms. "What do you want me to tell you?"

"Everything, Sweet Pea." She smiled warmly.

I parted my lips to speak just as our food arrived. The plates hit the table and I took in the scent of the pancakes. My mother quickly grabbed her silverware and dug in. She looked over at me and smiled. "Eat!" she exclaimed.

I let a breath escape and nodded, grateful to embrace something other than my thoughts.

Later that evening, I sat between my mother's legs while she parted my hair and applied coconut oil and curl cream to sections of my hair. I held the jars in my hands and listened to her ramble about everything and nothing. Robert Glasper's "In My Element" draped the living room like silk, and the sound of my mother humming along stirred a childlike comfort inside of me. A small smile hit my lips and I turned my head to look up at her.

"This makes me think about our house on Walnut Street, when you used to do my hair in the sunroom."

A light laugh glided between her lips. "You were so tender headed. I used to hate those mornings."

"Really? I loved them."

"You didn't act like it," she said softly. "It was a struggle trying to get you to come downstairs. I felt like I had to bribe you with Mickey Mouse waffles."

"It always worked."

My smile fell a little as the memory faded, replaced by the reality of where we were now. "I need you, mommy," I managed to say.

My mother stopped twisting. She held my hair in her hands and sat still. I waited for her to say something, but nothing came. She started to twist again before she gathered a scoop of cream to seal the twist.

"I feel like I've failed you, Nia. Like Nana failed me…"

I hadn't seen my Nana in at least a decade. Her relationship with my mother was fragile, prone to breakage. The two of them had a disagreement while my mother was in college and the relationship never recovered. With age, I grew to believe that the reason for their falling out was my father; my mother hadn't inherited Nana's gift of discernment. Nana hadn't trusted my father from the beginning, and when he turned out to be everything that she'd predicted, my mother resented her for it.

"That's not true," I said, before I swung around and sat on my knees, facing her.

Her porcelain smooth, butterscotch face had grown red with emotion and her eyes were glassy with tears.

"We've changed," she said.

"Some of it's my fault."

"Most of its mine. I should've called more, told you to come home more. Instead, I watched the distance grow between us when I knew that things were hard for you here. I should be here more. I don't want us to be like me and Nana."

"We won't be." I assured her of this, and crawled onto the couch to lay my head in her lap like the eight-year-old on Walnut Street. She scooped some coconut oil into her palm and grabbed another section of hair.

"Can't believe you're getting this beautiful hair braided next week," she said.

"...It's easier to deal with when I can put it away."

"The hair or everything else?"

"Both," I whispered.

***

The heart of the community I'd built at Monroe was my *Brown Girl* staff, but even with the fullness of black and brown sisterhood in that space, I craved the wisdom offered by my aunts back home. I sought mentorship to fill in the gap.

I didn't have many mentors during my time at Monroe. Just one – Dr. Lauren Ashworth, the dean of the Jansen College of Journalism. Our mutual love for black lives and journalism drew us close during my sophomore year. She'd grown up in the Midwest and had similar experiences of encountering race while situated in whiteness. We connected almost immediately – I was a reflection of her past, and she was a glimpse at my future.

She studied me from behind her tortoise shell frames one afternoon, before her eyebrows rose and her lips curled into a small smile. We were sharing tea at a local coffee shop for our monthly check-in.

"I read the latest edition of *Brown Girl*. I really enjoyed the piece on self-care. I must say though, Ms. Landrey, I miss your voice. You haven't written in a while."

I allowed my hands to curl around my mug of tea and nodded. "It's been hard Dr. Ashworth. When I sit down to write, nothing comes out."

"Something is in the way."

I nodded and let go of a breath I didn't know I was holding.

"Is it something I can help with?" she asked.

I'd set up this meeting to get her advice on writing the story about Jacob. Usually our meetings were about my professional future, but with Dr. Ashworth I grew to understand that the professional and the personal were inextricably linked. If I weren't so focused on keeping them separate, maybe I could write something.

"I heard about Mr. Moreland. He and I worked together last year when he was still part of student government. It's a pretty big deal for him to trust you with his story," she said.

"I don't think I can do it, Dr. Ashworth."

"The hardest stories to write are the ones you *must* write, Nia."

I'd heard this a million times from the professors I'd grown to value and appreciate during my time at Monroe. The sentiment was ideal, but it didn't make any of this easier.

"When you move through this world, anchored at your center and standing firmly in your truth, opportunities will present themselves. It's our call – it's our duty – to be driven by the truth. Give yourself the space to do this."

"Where do I start?" I asked.

She smiled and shrugged. "You'll know when you start. In the meantime, make some room upstairs." She tapped her head and offered me a smile.

"I'll try."

"And for what it's worth," she paused a little, before she rested her chin in the palm of her hand, "It's okay to not be okay. I just need you to own that."

"I'll be *fine*."

A reflexive response I'd gotten damn good at believing.

***

My stubbornness led me back to the computer and to my crippling silence. Nothing emerged and when the frustration boiled over, I slammed my laptop closed. I grabbed a notebook from my bookshelf, hoping to write down some ideas. Maybe with pen and paper I could start to push something out.

I scanned the pages of the worn notebook and stopped on the last entry. It was from the night I broke up with Quentin. My fingers traced the places where the ink bled through to the other side of the page – remnants of tears from that night.

Quentin moved to Washington, D.C. after he graduated from Monroe and we were in a long distance relationship for more than two years. I loved him as much as I could love, and I believed that – my heart grew to twice its size for Quentin and Quentin only. I adored him. I filled in all of his holes, sanded his edges and his rough parts, made him smooth and soft to the touch. He tried to do that for me too, but it never quite worked the same.

And then something changed. He and I weren't adversaries before but near the end, I made myself an enemy and drew lines in the sand. Love often felt like war to me. The internal battles I fought hardened me and made my relationship with Quentin a battle of its own.

I self-sabotaged. I self-detonated.

And he was collateral damage.

Eventually, I got tired of fighting my best friend.

The night that we broke up, I sat down in front of my laptop and called him through FaceTime. My heart raced as I held my hand over the mouse pad. I wanted to hang up but he answered before I could. He raised his eyebrows and lied back on the couch, before he scratched his head and tossed me a smirk.

"Did you call to apologize?" he asked.

"I want to break up. I'm done."

He furrowed his eyebrows – the thick, beautiful eyebrows I'd stroked and kissed so many times, hovered above his eyes, crumpled in confusion.

"What?"

His voice hurt like the sound of nails on a chalkboard and I cringed. I shut my eyes and stammered and stuttered. I couldn't bear to look at him and apparently I couldn't speak either.

"This isn't fair."

"I'm not my best self anymore," I whispered.

"And you think I'm the reason?"

He tried to *see* me through our digital distance, but the artificial view was the most disappointing part of all of this. He leant forward, almost like he wanted to caress my face, but I looked away and held back tears before I nodded my head.

"Yes."

I didn't mean that, but it was too late to take it back. He hung up on me that night and I hadn't heard from him since.

With the notebook in my hands and with three months between the two of us, I crawled into bed and grabbed my phone. Quentin's number was still saved because I didn't have the courage to delete it. When I called, he answered almost immediately. He was as stunned as I was. We sat in silence as I tightened my grip on the journal he'd gifted me last year for my birthday.

"Nia," he said finally.

The sound of his voice caused my wounds to crack open. I gushed from the inside out and he listened to me cry on the phone for a long while.

"I'm sorry," I managed to say finally.

"Don't apologize."

"Are you angry with me?"

"I was for a while," he said. "Are you okay?"

A small smile lifted the corners of my mouth. "I ended our relationship over the phone and you're asking me if I'm okay?"

"Why'd you call, Nia?" he asked. "It's been a few months."

"I need your advice," I said softly, before I sat up in bed and draped my arm over my knees.

I told him everything about Jacob's story and wanting to publish for *Brown Girl*; about my hair falling out and the writer's block. He listened before he offered anything.

"I wish you'd take better care of yourself."

"Quentin, don't start."

"I won't go there today. Anyway – thank you for trusting me with all of this. I think you know what you need to do. You have to write this story."

"For *Brown Girl*?" I asked.

"It's your platform. You started it years ago when I refused to publish a story that meant a lot to you. Things have a funny way of coming back around. Make the decision I didn't make."

"Thank you Q," I said softly. "…Can I see you soon?"

"I don't think so, Nia. Good luck with the story. I love you."

He hung up and I clutched the phone in my hand.

I waited for him to call back.

The call never came.

CHAPTER 12.

My mother never taught me how to braid. She could twist but she couldn't do cornrows. The first time I got my hair braided, the stylist added white and yellow beads to the end. I'll never forget the sound of those beads clinking against one another beneath my mother's large satin bonnet. I wore them to school with pride, only to be poked and prodded and made to feel different…and ugly. I begged for them to be taken down a few days later, and I wore my hair straight until I was eighteen.

To solve my breakage problem, Cecilia recommended a protective style and I fought her on it until I decided it was time to try something new. I feared for my edges – I'd heard things about the yanking from box braids. It was hour five in the salon chair and my leg bounced as I winced and whined. I slid my booty across that chair, trying to run from the pain. My neck grew tired of holding my head back and my eyes started to cross the longer I sat.

When I walked out of the shop with my neck stiff as a board, I got a text from Jacob. He was released from the hospital a few days earlier and he was jumping at the opportunity to meet me for an interview.

When we met, he wore his baseball cap low over his eyes and adjusted in his seat frequently. He complained of random aches and pains but apologized every time.

"Stop apologizing Jacob," I said finally, as I set up for the interview.

He studied me before he looked down at his hands. "I keep replaying the night over and over, wondering where I went wrong. I think it was my hands."

"What do you mean?" I started the recorder.

"I had my hands in my pockets."

"You did."

"That was a mistake."

"It was."

"My dad feels like this is his fault."

I allowed for a pause, hoping he would continue, but he stared at me blankly and waited for a follow-up question. The silence continued and he exhaled, slow and easy.

"We didn't have 'the talk'. I didn't even have an interaction with cops until I stepped on Monroe's campus."

"What's 'the talk'?" I asked more for the story I'd write than for me.

"You know...the talk. When a black mother or father sits down with an unsuspecting child and shatters their view of what it means to be free; when freedom becomes a figment of the imagination."

"I find that hard to believe, Jacob."

"What do you mean?"

"Your father *never* spoke to you about how to interact with the police?"

Jacob shrugged before he shook his head and sat back in the chair. He adjusted his leg once more and ran his hand over his knee. "He thought we were different – thought education and some wealth was enough to protect us."

"Protect you from what?" I asked.

"From blackness," he said softly. "I think my aversion to blackness grew from his."

He ran his hand over his knee and peered over at his reflection in the window. "I've never been so cognizant of my body. And not just because it hurts, but because I feel seen in a way I've never felt before."

I scribbled down a note and underlined it four times before I smiled over at him.

"Tell me about you – about home."

His parents worked hard to give him a life they didn't have growing up, so Jacob wasn't accustomed to cartoons and cereal on Saturday mornings. His weekends were packed with activities.

"My parents kept me busy."

"I see. And these activities, were they racially diverse?"

He smirked. "In a suburb of Boston? No. I was the diversity. I was the only black kid on my high school basketball team and I was captain. The only black kid in National Honor Society and the only black kid in most of my honors classes. I didn't know anything different. After a while, I don't think I noticed."

"What changed for you at Monroe?"

"Everything. After the incident with student government freshmen year and other shit on campus, my perspective started to change. I tried to join a few white fraternities last year, and that was an enlightening experience. As a black man, navigating whiteness and wealth at Monroe felt very different from my experiences back home. When that didn't work out, for obvious reasons, I started to think that it was time to seek community among folks who looked like me."

"And the night of the party you were seeking just that..."

He and I locked eyes before he swallowed the lump in his throat.

"I haven't slept much since that night. I keep mulling over the fact that we have to tell black boys where to put their hands in the presence of a cop," he said.

He leaned forward and put his hands over his eyes before I could see tears fall.

"I'm not angry anymore, just confused. My father looks at me like I'm the biggest mistake he's ever made. Like there aren't erasers big enough to rid him of the shame he feels and I don't know what to do with that. It's startlingly clear to him now that you can't raise a colorless child in America."

My lips turned down and I adjusted the recorder, watching him pull himself together. "You and I have argued so much about race these last few years. It's really hard for me to see you like this."

"It's all part of the process, right? The metaphysical experience of becoming black, of being black."

I stopped the recorder and smiled warmly at him, before I placed a hand over his.

"You did good, Jacob. Thank you."

***

Seventeen hours later, Jacob's interview was transcribed. The sun was extending its reach through the sky, and my neck hurt from hours of poor posture in front of my computer. I took off my headphones and sat back. I untied my braids and allowed them to fall down my back when I heard the shower start. Cecilia was awake. It was nearly seven in the morning.

I opened a new document and typed out a few words, before hundreds followed willingly. The fogginess in my head began to clear, and I wrote until I'd filled enough pages for the story. I crawled into bed after, welcoming sleep. My body felt lighter, physically and mentally, with the weight of Jacob's story behind me.

After what felt like a few minutes, I rolled over to the sound of my phone ringing. A glimpse at the clock shook me awake and I grabbed the phone to find Nicholas calling.

"Where were you today? You missed your presentation, Nia."

"I overslept!" I shrieked, before I hopped up and threw on clothes. Only I didn't have anywhere to go – I'd missed all of my classes.

"Meet me in my office in an hour if you want a grade."

He hung up the phone and I shook my head in disbelief before I snatched my laptop off of the charger and sprinted out of the apartment.

Nicholas was grading papers when I arrived. I was out of breath and drenched in regret and sweat. He didn't bother to look up, but allowed his eyes to dance toward the document I sat down in front of him. He picked it up and sat back in his chair before he stroked his chin and looked up at me from behind his reading glasses.

"You wrote the story."

I sat down and nodded. "I was up until nine this morning. That's why I missed your class. I'm so sorry, Nick."

My chest rose and fell as I attempted to catch my breath. He looked over at me for a while before he smiled a little. "I'm not giving you full credit. This is technically late."

"Completely understandable."

I opened my laptop and started my presentation. I hadn't practiced at all but I managed to finish in less than five minutes. He listened closely while he scribbled some notes on the rubric. He circled a grade and showed me.

"A C? Really?"

"Would've been a B if you hadn't slept through my class, Landrey."

"I guess something is better than nothing," I mumbled, before I packed up my things and went to grab the story. He stopped me from grabbing it and slid the story into his satchel.

"Let me hold onto this. I'll give you some feedback."

"Don't give that to anyone else," I warned.

"Or what?" he asked, before he smirked and went back to grading.

I sighed at the thought of my grade. "Your class will ruin any chance I had of going to graduate school. Thanks Nicholas."

"Stop whining." He laughed. "You've earned all of these shitty grades, and it's not because you aren't capable."

"I got a lot going on."

"Still dealing with the breakup?" He kept his head down and I fixed my eyes elsewhere, fighting the increasingly intimate moment as it went on.

"Sort of," I said.

"If you don't mind me asking, what happened?" He put his pen down and turned toward me. My eyes fell on him and he smiled a little and nudged his head, inviting me to open up.

"After the night of the party, I pulled away from Quentin. He'd call and I just wouldn't answer – couldn't answer. Didn't feel like talking. Got tired of *how are you* and *I wish you'd take better care of yourself.* Didn't want to hear about it anymore. Didn't want to deal with it. Just wanted to put it all away. When we did talk, I'd start fights. I was in a lot of pain, and I made him think that it was because of him."

"You pulled away from him when you needed him most."

"I needed me. I needed to show up for me and that hadn't been happening for a long time. I'm not very good at taking care of myself."

"Why's that?" he asked.

"I never learned how to."

***

Nicholas allowed me to turn in an assignment for extra credit in exchange for his feedback on my story. While he reviewed it, I spent a few nights in the library, napping and catching up on reading I'd missed this semester. Finals were right around the corner and I was in terrible shape.

After my third nap of the night, I heard my laptop chime and looked up to see an email from Nicholas. He sent me his feedback after reviewing my story, and he promised to return the story the following morning. I considered his thoughts before I made my own edits. I was finally ready to publish it.

The story would be published in the next issue, but when I got an email one evening from the regional chapter of the National Association for Black Journalists referencing Jacob's story, I knew that something was off. I was being considered for a grant for *Brown Girl*.

I read and re-read the email, before I packed up my things and walked across the quad to the sociology building. The snow started and a light dusting blanketed the campus. I left behind footprints as I climbed the steps to the building and peered over the railing to see the light on in Nicholas' office. It was after midnight. I called and stood outside in the cold while I waited for him to answer. Nicholas appeared at the door with a look of worry on his face.

"Nia, it's late. Is everything all right?"

I walked into the building and unwrapped my scarf. "What did you do with my story, Nicholas?"

He studied me before he walked toward his office without answering. I scurried behind him and smacked my lips as I pushed the office door shut.

"Nick?"

He sat down and looked up at me. "I sent an email to a colleague of mine at NABJ. I overstepped and I'm sorry, but this story is incredible. You're incredible. I needed you to know."

I sat down in the chair next to him and slowly rested against the back of the chair. My heart rate came down and Nicholas slid his chair closer to mine. His cologne was faint, the sign of a long day. He rested his elbows on the desk in front of him and my eyes traced his face.

"Thank you for the reminder," I said.

My voice seemed to echo, for the office was uncharacteristically quiet. My visits to his office were always shared with Coltrane or Monk. Without them playing in the background, I could hear our hearts beating in unison, a song that was just as beautiful.

Nicholas extended his arm across the back of my chair and leaned in toward me. Our warm breaths collided in front of us and I shut my eyes and placed a hand on his cheek. He slid his arm down the chair and placed a hand on the small of my back, before he pressed his lips against mine.

I allowed myself to unravel, and so did he. We pressed at each other's seams, as I fell captive to his touch. Palms to bare flesh, thigh to thigh, Nicholas filled in my gaps for a moment with something too tender for words.

CHAPTER 13.

My eyes fell on Jacob's empty seat as I made my way to my desk on the morning of my final for Nicholas's class. Jacob and his family decided to pursue a lawsuit against the university. We were one semester away from graduation, but he didn't enroll in spring classes. He was going home to Massachusetts and taking his tuition dollars elsewhere.

The pebbles in my stomach grew to the size of boulders as I anticipated Nicholas's arrival. The seats in the classroom filled up. Students ran through class notes from the semester, hoping to do a final review. My desk lay bare, with nothing more than a blue pen and regrets written in invisible ink.

The squeal of the door hinges sent my eyes to the front of the room. Nicholas walked in with a stack of freshly copied exams and went straight to his desk. He walked up and down the aisles, giving each of us our exams. The smell of his cologne drifted throughout the room, and I grew lightheaded as I curled my body toward the desk to avoid looking at him.

He went to the front of the classroom and watched us begin the exam. I could feel his eyes traversing me as I glanced from my desk to those around me. Everyone was moving through the test with ease and I was trying my best to remember what I crammed the night before. Midway through the exam, I put my head down on the desk. I prayed that I would pass, and I prayed for other things too – mostly forgiveness.

When the testing period ended, I was the last student in the room. Nicholas looked at his watch before he stood up and rested his hands in his pockets.

"Time's up, Nia."

I shut the exam and studied him from my desk. "I think I just failed your class."

He walked toward me and picked up the exam before he flipped through the pages and read through a few of my answers. He shook his head and stuffed the exam into a manila envelope with the others.

"You didn't fail, but you didn't do as well as you could've."

I put on my backpack and studied him. He was packing up to leave and my throat was on fire with questions that I wanted to shoot off at him. I walked toward him and swallowed, hoping to soothe my torched throat.

"Nicholas…"

"It was a mistake," he said coolly, as he put on his coat. He draped his satchel across his body and grabbed the exams as my eyes glossed over. I looked down at my shoes and blinked to stop the tears from falling.

"Which part?" I asked.

"I'll have your final grade up by Thursday. Good luck with your exams."

He turned on his heels and walked out of the classroom. I covered my mouth with trembling hands to conceal the scream that nearly fled from my mouth. Perhaps I was more embarrassed than heartbroken. Nicholas was the first person I'd willingly given myself to.

It was difficult to describe how I felt to Cecilia because I hadn't quite figured it out for myself. She rubbed my back as she and I sat on the thirteenth floor of the library. We were in the stacks, surrounded by dusty books. The concrete floor we shared made my butt raw the longer we sat with our backs against the shelves.

"Part of me feels betrayed…disposable…mostly stupid."

She took a sip of her tea and sighed.

"Have you considered going to therapy, Nia?"

"For what?"

I drew my knees into my chest and wrapped my arms around them, as my tired eyes took in the shape of my best friend.

"For everything. The assault, Quentin and now this, with Nicholas?"

"Nicholas was a one-off mistake."

"You might want that night with Nicholas to be a mistake, but I don't think it was. Our behavior always communicates something."

"I'm fine, Cecilia."

"No you're not, Nia!"

She put her hands up to her face and shook her head. "I need you to acknowledge your cracks. If you don't they'll become holes."

"What's wrong with a few holes?"

"I don't want you to have holes – I want you to be whole. But I can't want it for you more than you want it for yourself."

I let go of a sigh and laid my head back on the bookshelf. "I don't know what I need. My mother is in therapy, though. She's gone for years."

Cecilia smiled. "See, if your mom can do it, you can too."

I shook my head and stared up at the ceiling. "I don't want somebody digging up all of my shit, Cecilia."

"That's the work, Nia. You never know what you might uncover. Just try it out. We get free sessions through the university, so you might as well take advantage before we graduate."

***

I'd had dreams before about what therapy must be like. In the dream I wasn't in anything that resembled a counseling office. I was lying on an examination table, bare and uncovered. The blurry shape of a surgeon hovered above me, and he clutched a scalpel in his hand. I lied fully exposed and prepped for cutting. When the cuts started, they were deep and I felt them all.

That was my vision of therapy, and on the morning of my first session I couldn't shake the feeling that it would hurt more than a scalpel to flesh. I was lucky to be paired with a black woman. As I scanned the website the night before, she stuck out like a sore thumb. Not because she was the only black woman at the university's counseling center, but because she didn't smile in her headshot.

With my hands shoved into the pockets of a hoodie, I walked into the counseling center with my shoulders low and my eyes on the floor. I quickly scanned the waiting room, hopeful that I wouldn't run into anyone that I knew. The sign-in process was more extensive than I could've imagined, and as I scanned the list of boxes I could check – history of mental illness in the family, childhood traumas, molestations, *rape* – I omitted all of the sections and signed off at the bottom, before turning in the paperwork.

My eyes darted between the clock and the door. I considered leaving before the session started, and as I stood up to exit, a door opened revealing the black woman without the smile.

"Are you ready?"

I hesitated before I grabbed my belongings and scurried into the office. As soon as I crossed the threshold, I was consumed by the space. A candle sat in the middle of the room, filling my nose with what smelled like eucalyptus. The chair that I occupied curled around me like a cloud, as Dr. Johnson settled into her seat and offered me a glass of water. I declined. Her long sisterlocks draped around her shoulders.

"How's your day so far?" she asked.

Is this how therapy starts? With small talk? Sure, I can do this.

"Not too bad." I shrugged.

She studied me carefully, before she took off her shoes and sat with her legs crossed in her chair. "Tell me a little about you. I saw that you were a senior, studying journalism."

"I like to think that I'm already a journalist but it depends on the day."

"So on the days when you feel like you're a journalist, what's different?"

"I can actually write. I've been struggling to put words together lately. I had a small breakthrough a few weeks ago, but I haven't written since."

"I imagine that's frustrating for you."

"It is frustrating."

She paused for a long while, and I looked around the room, studying the walls when my eyes stopped on a picture of a baby – brown, with round cheeks and eyes the size of the moon.

"Is that your son?"

She nodded and turned around, admiring the photo. A large smile spread across her face – the first I'd seen since I met her ten minutes ago.

"Yes, that's him."

"He's handsome."

She turned back and traced my face with her eyes before she took a deep breath.

"What brings you in, Nia?"

Her voice fell. It was softer, gentler, as it traveled the space between us in the small office. I dropped my head and shut my eyes, as I clasped my hands together tightly. My heavy shoulders rose and fell with a shrug and she nodded.

"It's alright," she whispered.

I put my hands up to my face and I wept. And I didn't know why, but I didn't stop. Couldn't stop. The release felt like I was trapped in a tidal wave.

Like I'd been washed over.

Like I was drowning, and being pulled to shore at the same time.

CHAPTER 14.

I became more aware of the womanly shape I'd grown to fill. Glances at my reflection when I stepped out of the shower were longer now as I explored the contour of my hips – hips that refused to submit to jeans I once wore with ease and comfort. My chest was a nuisance now, blowing away buttons and bras with powerful protrusion.

The shape of womanhood came with more than discarded clothes and extended glances in the mirror. It came with yearnings that grew in size and intensity, like my hips.

I studied Cecilia curiously one evening as she lined her lips and sang to herself in the bathroom mirror. She wore a black jumpsuit that hugged her waist – it was her favorite date outfit. She was more curvy than I was, and shorter too. The long jumpsuit covered her feet as she stood up on her toes to apply liner to her bottom eyelid. The bathroom light above us flickered. Her perfume only slightly masked the smell of her conditioner as her damp curly hair rested against her shoulders.

"So this is date number three?"

"Date number three," she said, before she smirked at me through the mirror.

Cecilia had a rule that she applied liberally to her dating life: after three dates, she'd have sex with the guy she was seeing. I'd listened to her explain the rationale at least a dozen times, but figured I'd entertain the thought again.

"I thought you were lukewarm about this guy. What if you aren't ready tonight?"

"If I didn't think I'd be ready, we wouldn't be going out."

She puckered her lips and applied the deep plum lipstick she'd chosen before she looked over at me.

"Instead of poking holes in my dating philosophy, maybe we should work on getting you some action."

I shook my head and held up the book I was holding, a Terri McMillan book my mother left behind.

"I've got plenty of action," I said.

"Not living through the sex lives of fictional middle-aged black women."

She turned off the bathroom light and went into her bedroom to grab her clutch before she headed toward the door. She gave me a pitiful wave and left the apartment. I took a deep breath and rested my head against the wall. I turned over my wrist and looked at the time on my watch. It was a little after seven on a Friday night. I took a shower and shuffled through take-out menus. My phone lit up across the room. I had a new chat...from Nicholas. For a moment, I wondered why he'd chatted me instead of calling or texting.

Then I remembered: I'd blocked his number.

I fell back on the couch and studied the chat invitation before I accepted and watched his typing bubbles appear and disappear for what felt like an eternity.

Hey.

I stood up to consult Cecilia when I remembered that she wasn't home. The bubble appeared again and I sat down on the couch. I bit my lip and covered my eyes with my hands, when another chime came through.

Are you busy?

I sat the phone face down on the table and went back to the take-out menus. I stood there for a few moments, before I scurried back to the phone. I needed to know what he wanted – I *had* to know. He and I chatted back and forth for a moment, before he invited me to the sociology building to catch up. The moral minority in me thought that the idea was ludicrous. But the majority sent me out into the cold February night in a new pair of underwear I'd bought from Victoria's Secret.

***

"Nia, what are you doing?"

I repeated this to myself as I crossed the quad toward the sociology building. I stopped and turned around at least six times, as I imagined how this would go – how this would *look*! Stubbornly, I continued my pursuit, before I pulled the large, intimidating door open and stood in the foyer of the aged building. The sound of my feet on the cobblestone floor ricocheted off of the walls in the silent hall as I journeyed toward the only room with the light on.

My chest swelled as I stood outside of his office. The door muffled the sound of a trumpet, but the music blared in my ears when Nicholas' face was revealed. He froze in the doorway, and we stood staring at each other before he searched the hall behind me. He hesitated for a moment, his chest full of air, before he slowly deflated and pushed the door open a little more.

"Come in."

I walked into the office and he closed the door behind me. He wiped his palms on his jeans and stood with his back against the door. I walked to the other side of the room and removed my coat. Nicholas sat down across from me and watched as I thumbed through his books.

"I've never actually gone through these," I said.

He rested his elbows on his knees, before I looked over at him. He and I hadn't seen each other since finals week last semester.

"It's good to see you," he said finally.

The knots in my stomach untied themselves.

"You too. Can I have some tea?"

"Of course."

He stood up and grabbed a mug before he went down the hall to get some hot water. I slid my chair closer to his while he was gone and checked my lipstick using my cell phone's camera, before he walked back into the room.

"Pick your tea bag."

I stood up next to him and grabbed a bag of chamomile, as he and I tripped over each other's glances. A confident smile filled my face, and I slid between him and the desk. He looked down and took in the sight of me as he ran his hands down my arms.

"You made me feel really small before," I said softly.

"I'm sorry Nia," he whispered.

His breath, a mix of spearmint and chai, danced beneath my nose. He placed a small kiss on my collarbone and something that felt like fire – like lightning – danced up my legs. My mind grew cloudy as he and I unraveled again in that office. We undressed and I submitted to the yearning I'd learned to ignore. He fed my flames, and in that moment, I wanted to be set on fire as much as I wanted this – us – to be extinguished.

When the deed was done, so were we. He flicked on the overhead light, revealing the office for what it truly was. Under the guise of lust and nighttime, we'd gotten lost in a dusty old office that was much less attractive when it could actually be seen – when we could actually be seen.

The longing in his eyes as we said goodbye on the steps of the sociology building was a far cry from the regret I'd seen the time before. This felt final, but the flame still burned days after. At night, I tossed and turned and the space where my thighs met grew moist. I dreamt of he and I like we were a perennial flame; I dreamt of being burned.

I regretted our time together and I wanted to relive it all at once.

***

"You seem antsy today."

Dr. Johnson was perceptive. In the few sessions we'd had, she was able to read me better than anyone I'd ever known. I picked up her bowl of marbles for the third time and grabbed a handful.

"It's been a weird week. I'm frustrated."

"Frustrated about your writing?"

"No."

She raised her eyebrows and watched me sit the bowl down again. I sat back in my chair and crossed my legs. The shit with Nicholas wasn't comfortable for me to talk about, not even with Cecilia.

"I think my body is moving faster than my mind is."

She narrowed her eyes. "Is this about sex?"

I cringed at the word like a child.

"Are you sexually active? It's okay to share."

"Only recently."

I looked over at her and pulled my sleeves down over my wrists.

"You mentioned your ex-boyfriend before – Quentin. Were you sexually active with him?"

My eyes crawled toward her and I shook my head. "I couldn't."

"Couldn't?"

"Whenever I tried – *we* tried – I would stop him."

"Did that put a strain on your relationship?"

"He said it didn't but I believe it did."

"When you two were attempting to get physical, what kept you from going all of the way with him?"

"Fear."

"What were you afraid of?"

"Losing control."

"Of?"

"Of me – of my body."

"And things are different now?"

"Maybe. There's something seductive about the lack of control. Like I'm yielding to the waves… letting myself float," I said.

Dr. Johnson pursed her lips like she was choosing her words carefully before she leaned forward a little.

"I sense that there's some negative experience you've had with sex and control – something you've been fighting to overcome."

I smiled at little – a natural reflex – before I grabbed the bowl of marbles again. I held the cool marbles in my hand, and I clutched and released and clutched and released until tears were falling down my face.

She slid the box of tissue toward me and I snatched one.

"You're afraid of vulnerability," she said.

"Because I don't want to cry in front of you today?"

"It's bigger than that but we can't do the heavy lifting until you're ready. Right now you're defensive."

I dabbed beneath my eyes and took a few deep breaths – something she and I practiced last session.

"Remember where you are, Nia. This is safe. I'm safe. Be present with me."

"It's hard to do that when you're asking me to be somewhere else – somewhere that isn't safe."

"I understand," she said.

She sat quietly. I hated this – the silence she used during our sessions. It was her most effective tool. I'd gotten a lot from our dialogue, but I grew most during these moments of forced reflection.

"I was raped in high school," I said finally.

Hearing the admission aloud sent a jolt through my body and I looked at Dr. Johnson, waiting for her to respond.

"I'm sorry," she said.

"That's it?" I asked her. "I admit this huge thing to you and you...apologize? What are you apologizing for?"

Dr. Johnson shifted in her seat before she grabbed a journal from the bookshelf next to her. She started writing in the middle of our session, and I raised an eyebrow and shook my head. Maybe this was useless after all.

She ripped the piece of paper out of the journal and handed it to me. My heart swelled at the sight of two words: Me too.

We sat in an uncomfortable silence before I mustered up the courage to continue.

"How did you move past it?" I asked her.

Dr. Johnson usually avoided answering my questions. She told me that therapy was about me and for me; that she didn't want to take up space with self-disclosure. But today, she came and joined me on her small couch and draped one of her long legs over the other.

"Can I be transparent?"

I nodded, hoping that she would be.

"Similar to you, I couldn't have sex for a long time. But when I did...I did it a lot and I wasn't always safe or careful. I wanted all of my control back, and control for me was doing what I wanted when I wanted. I was in a very broken place but I've worked hard to be better than that version of myself," she said before she paused. "You may think that you are relinquishing some control, but I don't think you are. You've made a very conscious decision to have sex with someone who isn't Quentin."

"With Quentin, it was the nudity that I couldn't get past."

"What do you mean?"

"...The nudity," I paused, "I struggled to be bare with him. Not just in the physical sense, but emotionally too."

"Do you think Quentin loved you? Do you believe that?"

"I believe he did."

"Did you trust him?"

I looked over at her and nodded. "I did. A lot."

"Okay, let me ask something else. Did you believe that Quentin would always be there for you?"

"…Not if he saw the full extent of my brokenness," I whispered.

"You don't think he would've loved you regardless?"

"I'm not sure anybody would." *Not even me,* I thought.

"Tell me more about that."

"I think I always expected Quentin to get tired of me and my complexities so I pushed him away. I made things hard to see how he'd react…and then I left him first to beat the inevitable."

"Why are you convinced that Quentin would've left you, Nia?"

"Because men leave. They leave wives and daughters and the homes they've built. They make rubbish of royalty. They destroy women like my mother."

"This is about your father."

"No, it's about men."

"And that includes your father?"

"I suppose."

"You're still very angry with him for leaving you and your mom."

"…I'm angry with him for so much, but leaving me isn't it. I am who I am in spite of him."

"Tell me what you're angry about."

"Right now I'm angry about this conversation. I don't want to talk about my father. I didn't come here to talk about him."

"He's at the root of a lot of your pain, Nia."

I shook my head. "I don't agree. I won't let him have that type of hold over me."

"Your father is still in control. You can't run from this if you truly want to heal."

"I can," I said softly, before I grabbed my purse and stood up to leave.

CHAPTER 15.

I was always stingy with apologies. I would wait until I had something –
I mean *really* had something to apologize for before I would dish one
out. Dr. Johnson made the short list of folks I felt obligated to apologize
to, but she didn't accept it via text. She sent a calendar invite for our next
session instead, and at the session, she assigned homework.

I had to take out my braids.

"Why am I doing *that*? I don't understand this assignment."

"You will understand when you take them down," she said.

A few days later, beads of water rolled down my scalp as I saturated
each of my freed strands. I parted my hair into sections and pinned them
away, before starting the routine: shampoo, condition, and detangle. The
trashcan overflowed with clipped braids and hair lost from detangling.

In front of the mirror, I took in the sight of my bare, blemished skin.
My fro, free and full, hovered above me like a halo. The sun pushed
through the window like a spotlight, revealing dimples and stretch marks.
I studied every inch of myself in the mirror before a small smile
emerged. I could finally see myself.

"Confront your comfort this week," Dr. Johnson said before I left
that last session.

"That's why I started therapy," I'd responded.

I was standing near the door with my backpack on and she was
tidying up her office for her next session.

"There's more work to be done outside of here – work that I can't
do for you. You like to withdraw and retreat to your hiding place because
it's comfortable there. But the comfort you'll feel after you deal with the
things driving you to that place is the comfort we need to strive for."

I thought of Dr. Johnson's words as I walked out of the bathroom to
catch Cecilia in the hall. "Your hair looks really good. How was the
breakage this time?"

I raised an eyebrow. "Not too bad, actually. Maybe the protective
style did it's job after all."

Cecilia shrugged, scraping the bottom of her cereal bowl for the
sugar she'd added. "Or you took care of the hair underneath – can't

neglect it." She walked back into her room and I ran my hands over my hair, before the fro sprung back into place. I followed her and leant up against the wall.

"Would you be able to take me to the bus station this week?"

She raised an eyebrow, before she nodded and checked her planner. "Where are you headed?"

"D.C."

Confront your comfort, Nia.

***

In our relationship, Quentin made me his sun and rain. He wanted me to be the necessary condition for him to blossom into the type of man I needed. He planted himself in my soil, let his roots take hold. But after a while, we discovered that my soil was bad for planting, leaving both of us with little to harvest.

In his absence, the relentless winter cold clung to me. Seeking the warmth he'd bring, I boarded a bus without thinking about the possibility of failure, of being turned away, of never being forgiven. The ride to Washington, D.C. was a little over seven hours and when Cecilia dropped me off at the bus station Friday night, she handed me a bag of snacks and an Octavia Butler book.

I slept for an hour, before I sat awake in the uncomfortable chair on the Greyhound, writing and reading on and off. Time disappeared like we were in a black hole as the bus sped through the night. When we crossed the Maryland state line, I felt sick to my stomach.

This was a mistake.

When I visited Quentin last year, it was April. It was spring in the District and the cherry blossoms were in full bloom. He and I were walking near the Tidal Basin, when he stopped suddenly and peered down at our reflection in the water. I stood next to him and craned my neck to share the view.

"Sometimes we don't feel real," he said softly, before he turned and looked at me in a way that only Quentin could.

I wrapped my arms around his broad shoulders and rested my face against his neck. I breathed in his cologne and told him I loved him for the thirtieth time that day. One never felt like it was enough.

My glossy eyes could make out the shape of Union Station as the bus slowed and stopped. I slept at a hotel for a few hours, before I made my way to Quentin's the next morning. I walked swiftly through the chilly D.C. air, navigating with my GPS and taking in the neighborhood. The cultural shift – from Monroe's campus to Columbia Heights – was as remarkable as before when I visited. A small Dominican restaurant with Styrofoam take-out boxes shared walls with a chic coffee shop and a carryout playing go-go music.

I pulled my jacket closed and folded my arms as I neared the familiar row house. I pushed opened the aged gate that separated the cramped front yard from the sidewalk before traveling the small path that led to a side door. Suddenly, my mind flooded with potential scenarios. What if a woman opened the door? What if Quentin moved out before his lease ended? What if he didn't want to speak? What if…he did? What would I say?

I pulled out my phone to call him, when a voice startled me. My phone fell to the ground, and I looked up to see a sweaty Quentin standing on the sidewalk, staring at me with tears in his eyes.

***

Mornings with Quentin usually started the same way – an episode or two of "The Office," swapping headlines from our news sites of choice and omelets. Breakfast of champions, he called it.

This morning, he stood in the kitchen of his small English basement apartment and finished making an omelet for me. He slid the plate toward me without looking up. I stood up from the couch and grabbed the plate before I dug in and watched him. He'd slimmed down a little and when he turned around to pour me a glass of orange juice, I noticed that he'd grown out his beard. The two of us ate in silence before his eyes finally landed on me. His orbs were darker than before.

"Came a long ass way without calling first," he said.

"You would've told me not to come," I said.

"Absolutely."

I shut my eyes and nodded. "This isn't easy for me, just showing up like this."

Quentin twisted his lips to the side before he tapped his fingers on the counter. "When did you get in?"

"Last night. Stayed in a hotel."

He narrowed his eyes. "A hotel where?"

"My mom got me one. It was fine."

He shook his head and put our empty plates in the sink before I went and grabbed my journal. I ran my hands over it and opened up to the page where I'd written my list of apologies for Quentin. He turned around and noticed me reading.

"So why'd you come?"

"To apologize," I said softly.

"For?"

"For breaking up with you the way that I did. It wasn't fair to you and I'm sorry. I feel like I owed you more of an explanation. I said a lot of hurtful things to you because I was in a lot of pain. It's no excuse but…it's something."

He narrowed his eyes. "You reciting this from memory?"

"No," I said, before I shut the journal and tossed it on the couch behind me. "Quentin, I'm sorry."

"This is by far the most selfish shit you've done, Nia."

I furrowed my brow. "What?"

"To show up here with an unwarranted apology like my life's been on hold for you."

"I didn't expect your life to be on hold for me, Quentin. This was something I needed to do for me."

"Exactly – this shit has absolutely nothing to do with me. You could've stayed in Rhode Island and called. Maybe on FaceTime, or perhaps a text this time. Something more convenient for you."

He walked around me to his bedroom and I followed. I took a deep breath and shut my eyes. I was going to persevere through this conversation. I came too damn far on a raggedy bus that smelled like cigarette smoke and sewage. I had to try.

He pulled off his shirt, damp with sweat from his jog, and tossed it into the hamper. I pretended not to miss him as I stood in the doorway with my arms folded.

"Well I'm here so we might as well talk."

He looked over at me and chuckled before he shook his head. "You are something else. Still the center of everybody's universe, huh?"

"I'm the center of mine right now. I'm working through a lot of my shit and trying to take care of myself. Something you've always encouraged."

"Not at my expense, Nia! Are you doing some spring cleaning and figured you'd tidy up a bit? Show up on my doorstep and get in my way? I'm working through a lot of my shit too – and that includes setting firm boundaries with you and keeping you as far away from me as I can."

He picked up some clothes from the floor and threw them into the hamper before he grabbed his laundry basket and pushed past me to go to the laundry room. I stood with my back against the wall and wiped away the few tears that managed to escape. When he reemerged, he studied me before he plopped down on the couch and placed his hands over his face.

"It's hard to see you because I've tried to move on and get over the hurt you caused. But then you show up and..." He dropped his hands and looked up at me. "All I want is to hold you and make sure you're doing alright. I worry about you all of the time. The last time we spoke, you asked me if you could see me and I said no. I've thought about calling you every day since to say yes."

I went around to the couch and sat down next to him. "I pushed you away."

"You did."

"You weren't the source of my pain, but I blamed you for it. So much of this has been my own doing. I apologize – it wasn't fair."

"My job was to help you carry your burdens. I never wanted you to feel like you had to do that alone, but you wouldn't let me in. Wouldn't let me help. That's been the hardest part about all of this. I tried so hard to be there. We became so toxic and you just threw me away."

"There are parts of myself that I haven't learned to love. How could I expect you to do what I couldn't?"

Quentin's eyes fell on mine and we stayed there. He shook his head. "I tried," he whispered.

I looked down at my hands and nodded. "You did a damn good job being there for me. I didn't do my part and I'm sorry. I can't say it enough."

My face was wet with tears before I managed to smile a little. "It was good to know that somebody had my back," I said softly.

"I still do." He put his hand on my thigh and placed a kiss on my forehead. "Are you taking care of yourself?"

I let a laugh leave my lips before I wiped my face and nodded. "I can finally say that I am."

"It's hard to admit this but...I'm glad you came," he said softly.

"Me too."

CHAPTER 16.

In my final year of undergrad, there were lessons I'd learned through discomfort. The hardest one to grasp, but the first one to stick, was the inevitability of change. At times, I'd crumbled under the weight of transitions and change. Moments were finite and memories weren't enduring.

I'd gained so much in four years but I'd also lost a lot. The realization that this cycle of gains and losses would only repeat itself hadn't settled well with me. The losses tipped the scale – they felt heavier than the gains, and I was left in a perpetual state of imbalance.

I hadn't found my balance.

And therapy wasn't a sudden cure-all. I still had a lot to reconcile. I still had a lot of healing to do.

***

"So it's our last session. How do you feel?"

Dr. Johnson smiled and I sunk in my seat. The office didn't feel the same this time. There was an uneasy coolness, and the space that once brought me peace and comfort suddenly felt distant and unfamiliar. This was all over after today. I ran my hands along the arms of the chair I sat in and shrugged.

"I feel numb."

"Wasn't expecting that. You left our last session recharged and excited after your trip to see Quentin."

"I haven't seen you in a while. Things have developed since then."

"Things? Like what?"

"Quentin and I are going to try to be friends."

"That's exciting, Nia."

I rolled my eyes before I looked around the office, and folded and unfolded my legs in the chair. I couldn't sit still and neither could my thoughts; all of them raced around like tiny maniacs fighting for prominence. I had a lot left to say.

"It wasn't my choice. It was his. I wanted more," I said.

"It'll take Quentin some time to trust you again. You can't blame him for that."

"…I don't think I'm ready to end therapy. I'm not done yet."

"Tell me about that."

"I still have so much work to do and I need guidance. I'm graduating in a few weeks and I do not feel balanced – I'm not calm. I don't have a job, Dr. Johnson. My grades slipped this year. I lost the love of my life, watched a friend be beaten in front of me. The only thing that I've managed to keep up with is *Brown Girl*. I'm just not done – I still feel like I'm a work in progress. None of this has been easy."

"Who said it would be? This is the work we have to do – you're a woman, Nia. You have to put in work consistently to stay healthy – to thrive."

I folded my arms and shrugged. A smirk crept onto her face and she pointed to my hair – a dry, disheveled puff I'd shoved to the top of my head this morning and tied with a bow.

"It's like maintaining your hair. If you don't moisturize or get your ends trimmed, it'll be brittle, uneven and hell to deal with. Life is like that – you have to deep condition."

I turned up my face a little and she chuckled. "Why do you deep condition your hair?"

"It keeps my hair moisturized."

"And what else?"

"I think it repairs damage too. Oh, and it's good for preventing breakage."

She raised her eyebrows. "Deep conditioning in life is the self-work I need you to continue to do. Maybe it's therapy – or journaling. Maybe you need to start connecting with a spiritual center that reenergizes you. But the work doesn't end. I swear Nia, it's never ending."

I nodded as the message finally settled somewhere between my ears.

"…If I've gotten anything from you, and from these sessions, it's that a lot of the work I have to do has to happen when it's quiet. I think I've filled these last few years with a lot of words but very few of them were about me – or even for me," I said. I smiled at her from a place of true gratitude. "Thank you for encouraging me to love on myself a little bit."

"Don't stop," she said.

***

Cecilia had a job before graduation and she was moving to Seattle to work for a small tech start-up. She shared the news over dessert at our celebratory graduation dinner a few weeks later and I teetered between excitement and envy. I felt guilty about the latter, but smiled and ate through the discomfort that slid onto my dessert plate. She was my best friend and I wanted to support her.

Cecilia found a lot of success at Monroe. We'd walked different paths for four years – hers less bumpy, less tumultuous. A job before graduation made sense. She was incredible and she deserved it.

"That's great for Cecilia. I'm proud of her." My mother said one afternoon, before she looked at me. The inevitable pause immediately followed. "What do you think is next for you?"

"Mom, when I have a *next*, you'll be the first to know."

I was boxing up my clothes and I'd broken a sweat in the cramped bedroom. I stared at the wall that Cecilia and I shared for the last two years before my eyes welled.

"Can't believe it's over."

My mother grabbed another stack of t-shirts and tossed them into a box before she sighed and nodded. "Feels like just yesterday I was helping you move into your dorm. Now you're coming back home."

She and I locked eyes before she smiled a little and I winced at the thought. I felt like a failure. Going back home wasn't ideal. I wanted to write and I wanted to dream. Those two things – writing and dreaming – would die with me in Wisconsin if I went back. The despair on my face was clear and my mom pushed aside the cardboard box and patted the bed next to her.

"Can I tell you a story?"

"Ma, if this is the one about your first job interview, I can't take it today."

"I've never told you this one."

Her voice dropped a little and she turned her body toward me with her hands out, palms up. I joined her and put my hands over hers.

"After school your father and I moved into this tiny apartment in San Francisco. He was working at this community youth program and I was still dancing."

"It was the thirtieth of July when I found out that I was pregnant with you. It was hot as hell and I remember walking to the dance studio around the corner with my head in the clouds. I was so overwhelmed – I mean we were broke! Your father and I could barely keep the lights on. I decided to go dance. I could usually clear my head and calm down at the studio."

"I was moving for a few minutes. I managed to get through a sequence or two before I collapsed on the floor of the studio. I was rushed to the hospital and they ran a bunch of tests. They couldn't figure out what caused the collapse, but they advised me to avoid dancing for the rest of my pregnancy. That nearly killed me. Dance was my lifeline in the same way that writing is for you."

"After you were born, I had to take care of you so dancing for shows and practicing from sun up to sun down wasn't an option. I decided to teach instead – I could manage the schedule and take you to class with me some days."

"You and I are similar in our stubbornness. I know that coming home to Wisconsin is a letdown, but it won't end your career. You're just beginning, and dreams are amorphous – they shape shift. You'll find your way, even if the path you take isn't the one you planned for."

I rested my forehead against hers and nodded before she pulled me into her embrace. We wrapped our arms around each other until the uncertainty settled like dust. For a moment, the future felt safe and I felt...hopeful.

My phone vibrated against the top of the last piece of furniture I had yet to move out of my bedroom – an old side table my mother and father had in their first apartment in San Francisco. I looked up at the phone from the floor before I shut my eyes and let the call go to voicemail. To my aggravation, it rang again.

I sat up and grabbed the phone as it buzzed gently against my palm. An unfamiliar number with a 202 area code sat on the screen. I answered apprehensively and rested the phone between my shoulder and my ear as I stood up and walked out into the living room.

"Is this Nia Landrey? Sorry for calling on a Sunday – needed to catch you."

"This is Nia."

My mother was out grabbing take-out for dinner. My stomach hummed in anticipation as I stood at the window studying the sunset. There were a few moving trucks on the street below and students were packing their cars with boxes, ready to go home for the summer.

"Nia, my name is Vaughn Rhodes. I write for an online magazine based in D.C."

My body shot awake like I'd been in a deep slumber. I turned on my heels and faced the door. "Vaughn from *Pivot Magazine*? I just read your article on charter schools earlier this week."

"Great, you're familiar with us. I got your contact information from a colleague. He sent me a piece you wrote about the police beating at your school."

"What did you think?"

"I have a lot of thoughts but I am impressed. Not just with your technique but also with your ability to write something beautiful about America's Achilles' heel. Do you have plans after graduation? We want you to work with us."

I muted the phone before I jumped up and down until the soles of my feet were raw.

"I don't have plans. Nothing secured right now."

He and I set up a Skype interview and my hands shook as I wrote down all of his contact information. This didn't feel real. My mom returned with food in her hands as he and I were ending our conversation. She stood in the bare living room and watched me scribble notes on a receipt I'd found in my back pocket.

"Before you go, would you mind telling me who shared the piece with you?" I asked.

He hesitated for a moment. "He didn't want me to tell you, but it was Quentin Moore. He speaks very highly of you."

After I hung up I exhaled, deep from the gut and a big smile filled my face.

"Change of plans, Ma!"

Part III.
Twenty-Six

CHAPTER 17.

I got a good look at my mother a few days before my twenty-sixth birthday. Crows left footprints at the corners of her eyes and gray hair sprung from her temples like her thoughts had aged her. She'd hung up her dancing shoes a decade ago, but that day she bent her body in ways that only a dancer could as she helped me maneuver a new couch through narrow hallways and doorframes.

The two of us moved furniture around in my apartment until the room felt full – an impossible task. In my twenty-fifth year, I'd discovered that there were empties that expensive rugs and bank accounts couldn't fill. The kind of empties that drew sad calls from my mother on birthdays now – calls with pregnant pauses, calls about calls unanswered.

On my twenty-sixth birthday, I received the call that I didn't want, the call that she didn't want to make. But here we were. It was a little before three in the morning when my phone rang. She was back in Wisconsin so a call at this hour felt out of place.

"Mom it's late," I answered, my voice hoarse.

"Happy birthday, Sweet Pea."

I ran my hands over my face. I sat up in my bed and braced myself. "When did he pass?" I asked.

"An hour ago."

I responded with silence. I could hear my mother sniffling on the other end and I stood up to go to the living room. I sat down on the couch, lied back and looked up at the ceiling. Lights from passing cars made shapes appear and disappear on the walls and my mother's sniffling became unbearable.

"I've gotta go," I said. I draped my arm over my forehead and allowed a deep sigh to escape. "I'll call you in a few hours."

"I'm sorry, Nia."

I hung up the phone and tossed it onto the coffee table before I stood up and went into the kitchen to grab a bottle of whiskey I hadn't opened yet – a birthday gift from Cecilia. I took a shot from the bottle and scoffed as it burned my throat. I grabbed the bottle by the neck and took more sips until I couldn't feel the burn – until my throat was numb.

Until I was numb.

A loud snore startled me awake and I sat up on the floor of my living room next to Grant sleeping peacefully. I studied him before I crawled to the couch and grabbed my phone. It was nearly three in the afternoon. Grant rolled over and hit his head on the floor.

"Shit," he mumbled, as he sat up and yawned. "Why did we decide to sleep on the floor again? Too old for this, Nia."

I pointed to the empty bottle of whiskey and held my head. "We're too old to be drinking like fish too," I mumbled. I'd called him at five a.m. slurring my words. I didn't ask him to come over but he showed up forty-five minutes later with chocolate. We drank until we both passed out on my floor.

Grant's eyes curled around me, before he pulled his knees into his chest and draped his arms over them. "Want to go for a run?"

"No thanks," I said, before I lied on the couch and covered myself in a throw blanket. "I need to be alone today."

"Are you sure?" he asked. "I'm good all day, just got some grading to do later."

"I'm fine. Thank you for coming by last night."

He nodded before he stood up and kissed my forehead. He grabbed his hoodie and pulled it over his head. "Call me if you need anything. Happy birthday, beautiful."

I shut my eyes and the door to the apartment closed. I lied on the couch until the sun went down again. I slept on and off. Woke up and fell back asleep because being awake was too painful. My phone vibrated from the floor at seven and I ignored the call because it was my mother...and then Grant...and then Cecilia.

Vaughn called next.

"Is this work related?" I asked, wiping my hand over my face and sitting up. It was well after ten at night. "It's Sunday night."

"Happy birthday again. Sorry to bother you," he said. "You sound like shit."

I felt like it, too. "What do you need?"

I grabbed my planner and opened it up, turning to the week ahead. A ton of meetings, interviews, and edits. This was the worst time to bail on work.

"I checked your calendar. I know you have to interview that wellness blogger on Wednesday, but I'm going to get Christina to do it. I've got a new project I need your help with," he said.

"I've gotta take the week off, Vaughn." I sighed and tossed my head back. "Going home."

"Home?" He chuckled. "Like Wisconsin?"

"Like California."

He paused before he made the connection. "Nia, I'm so sorry. If I'd known, I promise I wouldn't be calling you about work. Are you good? Do you need to talk?"

"The last thing I want to do is talk. Skype me into meetings this week. I'll be available, but I'll let you know when I can't be."

"No, you're done. I'm clearing your schedule and emailing HR right now about bereavement leave. This isn't optional."

"Are you my friend right now or my boss?"

"Both. I'm so sorry for your loss. Get some rest. I'll see you in a few weeks."

We ended the call and I took a deep breath and lied back on the couch as I allowed myself to cry.

"You asshole," I whined. "Died on my birthday."

I sent my mother a text, asking her for details about his arrangements before I booked a flight to California to bury my father.

He'd bid me adieu with one final selfish act.

***

How do we prepare for grief? There's no training, no conditioning, to get your heart in shape for a marathon of this sort. And grief for my father felt strange.

He looked a lot like my grandmother so she and I were nearly identical. I remembered this when we arrived at her house the night before the funeral. She opened the door and gasped a little when she saw me standing on the steps of her Oakland home. She grabbed my hands and smiled up at me. Her small, feeble frame invited me inside with her arms wrapped around my waist.

My mother shut the door behind us and grabbed some tissue from her purse. She wiped her tears and walked around the living room. "Looks the exact same, Annie."

My grandmother was a woman of few words – I remembered this from stories my mom told me. We'd only seen each other twice: a Christmas I spent with my father when I was five and on my seventh birthday. Nineteen years later I sat on the floor in front of her like a child, marveling at her timeless beauty.

She rocked in her chair and asked us a few questions – small details she hoped to string together. We were all familiar strangers, much like my father and I. I stood up and looked at the framed photographs she kept on the mantelpiece. I stopped on a picture of my father holding me with cotton candy in my hand. I ran my fingers over the photo before I turned and looked at my grandmother.

"Can I have this one?" I pointed to the picture.

She nodded and smiled. "It's yours."

I took the photo out of the frame and slid it into my planner before I signaled to my mother that I was ready to leave. I had a lot to think about before tomorrow – before saying goodbye to a man I barely knew.

When we got to the funeral the next day, I hung close to my mother. We held hands as we ascended the steps of the large church. I learned the night before that this was his church home in his latter years.

My mother and I walked down the aisle toward the casket among parishioners and distant family. I looked around at the others, wondering how their lives intersected with his. I held my breath, my stomach clenched tight. I held onto my mother's arm and shut my eyes. "No," I whispered to her.

"Just a few more steps honey," she said. She wept as we approached him and I stood frozen, erect with fear. I studied the mahogany casket before I allowed my eyes to fall on him.

The first time I saw a dead body I was eleven. My uncle died and my mother and I drove to California to attend the funeral. I remember peering into the casket and getting an eerie feeling. He didn't look like himself and that terrified me. As I stood in front of my father, I realized that I didn't know what he looked like before he died. I couldn't even make the comparison.

I lingered for a while, in a trance-like state. I thought about throwing my arms on top of him, thought about cursing his name. I imagined the moments before he took his last breath – did he think of me? I hoped that he smiled before he went. I really did. My mother called my name and I touched his chest with a trembling hand before my knees buckled. I fell into my mother's arms, and I cried as she carried me with the bit of strength she had left.

After the funeral, my mother entertained condolences and well wishes from people who once knew her. The congested sidewalks caused my chest to tighten and I watched the hearse disappear down the street. I wrapped an arm around my mother as she checked her make-up. A light wind lifted her straightened strands and she pushed the hair behind her ear to keep it out of her face.

The sun was blinding. There wasn't a cloud in the sky. I squinted, holding a hand over my eyes when I saw Cecilia approach. She walked up carrying a fussy Justine on her hip and I smiled a little.

"Baby girl," Cecilia said, before she reached for a hug.

I hugged her tight and kissed Justine's forehead. Baby Justine touched my cheek and studied her little fingers, wet with my tears. She'd just turned two years old a few days earlier. Cecilia hugged my mother before her husband came around with Justine's diaper bag.

"Nia, how you holding up?" he asked.

He and I embraced before I shrugged. "Ready to get back to work," I said softly.

Cecilia sighed. "I think you need more than a few days off Nia,"

I brushed past her statement and forced a smile. "Congrats on the new job, Supermom." I smiled. They'd recently moved to Sacramento for Cecilia's new job. In four years, Cecilia managed to build a family and a career – two things I hadn't done. We were as close as we could be, despite her growing demands.

Cecilia's husband went to get the car and my mother cleared her throat. "Beautiful family, Cecilia. I'm proud of you," she said.

Cecilia glanced at me and I put on my sunglasses and looked out toward the street. At Cecilia's wedding two years ago, my mother wept audibly in the third pew. She was the loudest in the room and the only person who looked visibly upset. I cut my eyes at her from the front of the church and approached her at the reception. She and I got into our first real argument about my future before Cecilia's brother intervened. We hadn't ever processed the event, but I internalized a lot of what she said that night. She projected many of her failures on me and made me feel like I wasn't good enough – wasn't *as good as* Cecilia.

Standing in front of the church with them now, I shook off the thought and kissed Justine's forehead. Cecilia hugged me before she left.

"I'll call you this week. I love you."

When they left, I looked toward the church once more. A woman exited the church and headed down the steps in my direction. I handed my mother the shawl she'd worn to the funeral. "Let's get some food."

"Nia," the woman called.

I looked over my shoulder and furrowed my brow as the woman neared. She was still dainty but she'd grown curvier with age. The cheekbones my father gifted her were hidden beneath blush and freckles I didn't know she had.

"It's been a long time," she said.

I studied my sister before I nodded. "It has. At least ten years."

"Nana told me that you're out in D.C. I thought about reaching out, but I wasn't sure you would want to hear from me."

I looked down at my hands. "I haven't wanted to hear from you. That has nothing to do with you, but everything to do with him."

"I know," she said softly. "Will you take my number? You don't have to call, but if you ever wanted to, I'd like to get to know you."

I hesitated before she and I exchanged information. My mother rubbed my back as we walked back to the car. She looked over at me and smiled.

"How do you feel?" she asked.

"Exhausted. I just want to eat and watch trash TV with you at the hotel."

"Sounds like heaven." We shared a laugh. It felt good to laugh.

***

I flew to Wisconsin with my mother after the funeral. A visit was long overdue – I hadn't been home since Thanksgiving. When we pulled up to the house, there were a few boxes on the steps.

"What did you order?" I asked as I got out of the car.

"I didn't order anything," she said as she neared the steps.

She'd gotten a few bouquets of flowers. She smiled a little and hoisted them inside. I dragged our suitcases over the threshold and shut the door as she turned the heat up and took off her coat.

"Who sent you these?" I leant down and opened one of the boxes, revealing a beautiful bouquet of chrysanthemums.

"Mommy look at these!"

She walked into the living room carrying a bottle of wine and two glasses. She raised an eyebrow. "I've never liked those but you love them. Read the card."

I pulled the card out and my smile faded. She sat the bottle down and read the card over my shoulder before she chuckled. "That was my first thought when I saw those ugly things. He used to buy them for you, right?"

I rolled my eyes and stuffed the card back in the envelope.

"I thought you two were on speaking terms again," she said.

"Something like that," I sighed.

How did Quentin find out about my father? I pondered the thought for less than a moment – Cecilia.

"This was thoughtful. I'll be sure to give him a call."

"Spare me the details when you do."

I sat down on the couch and propped my feet up. She and I tapped glasses and settled into the evening we'd share – a beautiful rarity. She rested her forehead against mine and smiled, "So glad to have you home for a little while."

***

The visit was short lived. I was on a plane to D.C. three days later. A nearly identical bouquet of chrysanthemums waited for me at the concierge's desk when I got back to my apartment. I considered leaving them downstairs, but I grabbed them begrudgingly and left them on a side table near the door.

I was up by 5:30 the following morning and every morning to beat the sun. As soon as I got out of bed, I listened to the news highlights from the previous day while my coffee started. Shower, make-up, and outfit for the day; bagel by 6:15. Most days, I pushed my hair up into a puff, my edges laid flat with gel and a prayer.

With my iPad cradled under my arm and my bagel between my teeth, I shuffled to the door with one shoe on and the other in my hand. The sight of the chrysanthemums caused me to shudder. I tossed them down the trash chute on my way to the elevator.

Once outside, my fingers slid up and down my phone as I checked Twitter and scurried to the metro station. I loosened the top button on my shirt and draped my cardigan over my arm. Drops of sweat assembled on my temples as I walked – the sign of a humid day already. As I entered the metro station, I noticed a woman and her child sitting near the top of the escalator. The woman and I were familiar. I was in a rush one morning, running late to work when I dropped my wallet. She ran after me for a few blocks and returned it to me. I ended up being late to work anyway, after insisting that I buy her breakfast.

This morning, she held out a tattered McDonald's cup with her daughter standing next to her. "Good morning," I said softly.

I approached the two of them and pulled out my wallet. I found a few dollar bills and slid them into the cup.

The woman smiled. "God bless you, sis. Good morning."

I looked down at her daughter, noting her big, almond-shaped eyes. She dragged her feet across the concrete and looked up at me.

I smiled a little. "I like your dress, sweetie," I said softly.

"Thank you," she said. She turned away from me as she gripped her yellow dress and hugged her mother's leg.

I walked into the station and as I descended on the escalator, I saw my train arriving. "Shit!"

I tried to sprint but with heels and a million bags, I only managed a jog. I made it on the train just as the doors were closing. When I got to *Pivot*, Vaughn's office light was on. I peaked my head in.

"Why are you always the first person here?" I asked.

"First to arrive, last to leave. The better question is why the hell are you here? You're not due back for another week."

He hopped up and walked to his mini-fridge before he grabbed an apple juice and offered me one. He leant up against his desk and popped it open.

"I need to work," I said. "Where are you going today?"

Even for a Friday, he was dressed casually, with a lightweight sweater that clung to his arms, tapered khakis and low, slip-on sneakers.

"Got a lunch date." He winked as he went back to his chair.

I walked into the office and smirked. "Is this with the doctor?"

"Affirmative," he said softly.

"Don't play it cool! You're excited."

"I'm not excited, that's a meaningless emotion. However, I am hungry and he's paying."

I rolled my eyes and headed toward the door. "Well bring me back a doggy bag, or a friend of your doctor friend."

"You have a man."

"Can you stop?"

"I'll stop when you stop," he said, before he cut his eyes at me. "Welcome back. You look well."

I smiled at him and went down the hall to my office. There were a ton of flowers lining the walls and cards scattered on my desk. I stood at the door and dropped my bag on the floor as my shoulders slumped forward. I couldn't wait until this part was over, couldn't wait for things to be normal. My office was the size of a large closet but it was a step up from the cubicle I'd claimed for two years. I was thankful for the window – and a door to shut when I needed to.

I busied myself with emails for most of the morning, before I cleaned the office and shoved all of the flowers into a corner.

Later that morning, Vaughn knocked on the door and I held my breath, hoping he wasn't coming to check on me. He raised an eyebrow. "I'm pulling you into a meeting with Abbi and I this afternoon."

I smiled and bit my lip, before I nodded and wrote a post-it to remind myself to prepare during lunch.

"Are you pitching a story?" I asked.

"You're pitching a story. I just sent you an email. I'm setting the ball, I just need you to strike."

"Consider it done."

Vaughn winked and left the office and I sat down, eager to read his email and get to work. I'd be working through lunch and the thought brought me joy. Finally some normalcy, some competency. I couldn't always do feelings, but dammit I could write.

***

You could get lost in Abbi's office. She managed to squeeze an entire library collection into the small space. My eyes traveled between titles she stacked on top of each other in neat piles.

"The books are like my limbs. They're an extension of me now." She let a light laugh escape while we waited for Vaughn to join us. Abbi's face was round but her high cheekbones and contoured face added a sharpness that felt out of place. She was fair-skinned with short hair that she'd recently dyed red. Her soft voice – rarely heard on the other side of her office door – quieted my nerves as I prepared to pitch.

Abbi was a D.C. native. She'd recently started at *Pivot* as our Managing Editor for the Race and Culture department. Within her first week, she promoted Vaughn to Associate Editor. I was gunning for the open staff writer position, but I hadn't had time to pitch to Abbi yet. In my current role as Editorial Assistant, I wasn't the first person she'd select to write.

"I won't stay very late. I've got to grab my daughter from school," she said, glancing at the time on her watch.

Vaughn walked in and shut the door before he smiled a little at me and pulled a chair up to Abbi's desk.

She ran her tongue across her teeth and rested her elbows on the desk. She lifted her eyebrows and looked between the two of us.

"So what are we pitching?"

I looked at Vaughn and he looked back at me, waiting for me to begin.

"Oh." I stammered before I opened up my notebook.

I'd worked with the Race and Culture department for more than three years but the journey had been slow. I was more of a copyeditor than a writer for our team. And even when I contributed to a story, I rarely received a byline.

Abbi stopped me in the middle of my pitch and smiled. "I think I get the gist. I'll follow-up with Vaughn to see if it's worth pursuing. Thanks, Nia."

I was terrible with feedback – constructive and critical – but no feedback was worse. I looked at Vaughn and he gave me a reassuring head nod before I got up to leave. I went back to my office and engaged in more self-deprecation than was healthy. I considered staying late – to work on more pitches, to redeem myself. But before I could commit to that, I got a text from a number I hadn't saved.

Can I feed you?

CHAPTER 18.

Dating in the District? It was the best of times and the worst of times. I'd underestimated the complexities of adult relationships in the social media age. On my quest for a genuine connection, I found a bunch of online personalities that didn't translate to anything substantial in real life. I tried "swiping right" and "sliding in DMs," but none of it felt organic. I hadn't dated since Quentin. He'd been the co-author of my love narrative – a narrative that seemed unrealistic now.

There were plenty of nights I'd spent in the company of others but few were meaningful in the morning. I'd taken a break from dating for a few months when I met Grant.

I was on a rooftop after work with a glass of wine in my hand, swaying to the sounds of The Foreign Exchange. The sun was going down and so were our inhibitions as drink tabs increased and the dancing got less formal. My friend from work, Joyce, tapped my shoulder and nodded her head toward the other end of the bar.

"Don't look, but dude in the blazer hasn't stopped looking at you since we got here."

"Don't look? Why?" I quickly glanced down the bar and he and I locked eyes. "Oh, you're right."

"Could you be more thirsty? I told you not to look. Now he's walking over here. Finish your drink so that he can buy us a round."

"Us? What is wrong with you?"

She smiled a little and tossed her glass back, leaving the ice cubes and her shame behind.

"What are you drinking?" he asked. His voice sent a chill down my back and my eyes rose to meet his as he leant up against the bar and studied me intently. The heat between us was apparent immediately.

I raised my eyebrows and Joyce smiled and stuck out her hand. "She started with a malbec but I think she was eyeing the whiskey selection. I'm Joyce."

He shook her hand and looked back at me. "So whiskey?"

"Whiskey's fine," I said.

He ordered me a drink, and one for Joyce too, much to her delight. She bounced away and left me with the cool stranger. He had an easy smile with beautiful teeth and light dimples. On its descent, the sun doused him in oranges and pinks, flattering his dewy, caramel skin. I played hard to get for a while before I gave him my phone number. He was quick to call after we met. Grant wasn't the type to play coy.

Our first date was a Nicolay concert and we danced from Shibuya to Soweto, soaked with sweat. Outside of the Howard Theater, he kissed me while I waited for my Uber and he made plans to see me again. He was future-oriented and clear with his intentions. The two of us hadn't seen eye to eye on either.

***

Grant's apartment was warm like him. He'd recently moved to Columbia Heights and the small one-bedroom apartment fit him like a glove. I dropped my bag near the door and placed my shoes on the mat next to his – a line of wingtips in various colors. He'd unpacked another box of books and they were stacked on the coffee table – *Americanah*, *Between the World and Me*, *The Alchemist*. I sat down on the large, brown leather couch and fingered the titles. I opened a few of them, studying his notes in the margins. Grant walked out of the kitchen in a hoodie and sweatpants with a dry towel on his shoulder. He smiled and kissed my cheek.

"What we drinking tonight?"

Various aromas swirled in the apartment, making my stomach sing. "Something stiffer than water," I said, suddenly noticing the music he played – Braxton Cook's "Somewhere in Between."

When he returned from the kitchen with a goofy grin on his face, I gave him a side eye and took a sip of his creation. "This tastes dangerous."

I joined him in the kitchen and watched him prepare our dinner. "When are you going to teach me how to cook like this?" I asked.

"When you break up with your take-out menus," he responded.

"Wow that's shady. I've made breakfast for you before."

"An omelet," he corrected, before he started to put our food on plates. He took bread out of the oven and brought a salad to the table. We ate and swapped stories about our workweeks. I laughed until I needed stitches and drank until my head felt light.

"One more of these drinks and I'm sleeping here tonight," I said.

We'd retired to the carpet. I sat with my legs draped over his as he rubbed my feet and listened to me ramble. I grabbed one of his books – *How to be Drawn* by Terrance Hayes. He watched me review the poems he'd marked up, one much more than the others – "New York Poem."

"This one must be your favorite," I said.

"I love the part about contranyms – it reminds me of you."

I reviewed the poem before I found the line he referenced. I frowned a little.

"How so? How does *bolting* remind you of me?"

"Well, as he states, bolt can mean to lock and to run away, and...you're good at both."

I studied him, wondering how he knew me so well, so quickly. I put the book back on the pile and leant back on my hands.

"Are you staying?" he asked.

"I'd like to."

We did this dance every time I came by for dinner. "I made some room for your things in the top drawer."

I tensed up. "Why are you sharing that now?"

"Because I need you to know that this isn't casual, Nia. This is the fourth time in two weeks that you've stayed over. You bring by a toothbrush, leave earrings behind. What should I make of that?"

I shook my head and looked away from him. He smiled a little and pulled me closer, pressing his face against mine. "Which *bolting* will you do tonight?"

"Neither," I whispered, before I pecked his lips with my eyes open and got a good look at him. He caressed my back, placed a kiss on my neck and allowed his warm breath to hover there. My body responded and he laid me back on the high pile rug I'd helped him pick out at Ikea. He was slow and soft – patient and responsive. We made love on the floor between stacks of books.

When the sun danced across my face the next morning, I woke up tangled in his sheets. I touched my dry hair – I'd forgotten to wrap it up the night before. Grant was at his desk, cradling his coffee mug and reading the *Washington Post*. I watched his shoulder blades move as he raised the mug to his lips.

"Good morning," he said softly, his eyes on his laptop.

I stood up and wrapped the sheet around me before I walked to him and kissed the top of his head. "Busy day today?" he asked.

"Yeah I should jet," I said as I walked into the bathroom attached to his bedroom. He sat back in his chair and watched me as I turned on the faucet and examined my skin in the mirror.

"You got work to do?" he asked, trying to discern why I needed to leave. I didn't have a reason – just knew I couldn't stay.

"Some work to do…yes," I said before I dropped the sheet and turned on the shower. I shut the door behind me and Grant resumed his sipping. When I was done showering, I threw on some clothes and gathered everything that I could remember to grab. Grant stayed at his desk and when I kissed the top of his head, he didn't move. Didn't bother to walk me to the door, either.

Before I left, I hesitated for a moment. I gripped the doorknob and looked around the living room. I imagined us on the couch and on the floor, laughing and eating again. I pulled myself back from the reverie and cleared my throat.

"I'll talk to you soon," I called to him.

No response.

When I left, I lied on my living room floor and ate peanut butter from the jar. Grant didn't call for the rest of the day and that bugged me. I was trapped in a game of tug-of-war, but I was playing myself.

"Call that man Nia," Cecilia said that night on the phone.

"I just left this morning. Don't wanna go running back," I said softly as I looked down at a busy Florida Avenue from my living room window. Cecilia shushed a cranky Justine and sighed.

"I don't understand your stubbornness. He's been around for how long now?"

"I don't know...six months or so."

"Six months? Nia, are you crazy?"

"I'm not crazy."

"Well are you seeing other people?"

"No."

"Then what?"

"You know what, Cecilia. I'm not ready."

"I need you to get over that Quentin shit like yesterday."

I looked down at my hands – at my bare ring finger and bit my bottom lip.

"Quentin asked for my address when I called to thank him for the flowers."

"Is he inviting you to his wedding?"

"I think so," I whispered.

"You should've said no."

"I regret speaking with him."

"Well you don't have to go to the wedding. Just send them a gift, wish them well and move the hell on with Grant."

"Why bother? We'll probably end like Quentin and I."

"I'm not doing this with you. Call that man, Nia."

She hung up the phone and I stared at it until the screen went black. I poured myself a glass of wine and lit some candles before I went to my desk and sat down to get some work done. My apartment was on the top floor of a four-story building. Many of the units were renovated, but they kept the original hardwood floors. I sipped the wine and studied the eggshell-colored walls in my living room. There were four cans of paint stacked in the hall, but I hadn't touched them. I bought them the day before my birthday – the day before I found out that my father died. My motivation to "spice up" the apartment, to make it feel like home, disappeared that day.

I could hear car horns and loud music on Florida Avenue as people waded through thick traffic, heading to bars on U street. I turned toward my laptop, put on my headphones and sunk into Gretchen Parlato's voice. I finished up a project I was helping Vaughn with before falling asleep with my head on the desk.

***

Grant hadn't called in a few days. I got a little nervous when Wednesday came and went without a word from him. I listened to Pandora during my evening commute and when Nicolay came on, I decided to ride to Columbia Heights. I scurried across 14th street and slipped into Grant's building as a tenant held the door open for me. Standing outside of his apartment door, I raised my hand to knock but I hesitated. I thought about turning around when I heard the lock click. Grant pulled the door open wearing workout clothes. He furrowed his brow and took out an ear bud.

"You cool?" he asked. "Everything alright?"

I nodded and swallowed, my mouth suddenly dry and without words. We stood in silence for a little while before he pushed the door open and allowed me to walk inside. I took off my jacket and hung it up on a hook near the door before I turned and opened my mouth to speak.

"Save it," he mumbled as he walked down the hall.

I followed behind him and stood at the door of his bedroom. I dug deep for an apology before I shut my eyes and sighed.

"You're upset with me but I haven't heard from you either," I said.

He looked across the room at me before he shrugged. "Because I'm done doing this with you. We're too old."

"Doing what, Grant?" I whined.

"This! I can't be in this by myself and you and I both deserve better than this little dance we've been doing. Maybe you should figure some shit out on your own and keep me out of it."

I parted my lips to speak but settled for a slight shrug instead. Grant watched me fuddle around in my silence before he chuckled. "Incredible."

"I'm sorry!" I belted.

"For what?" he asked. He sat down on the bed and stared at me.

"For...bolting. For making this hard for you."

I sounded like a broken record. I'd given this speech at least a dozen times with Quentin, until he was finally fed up with my antics. Grant appeared to be close.

"...I'm really close to loving you and that scares the shit out of me," I said. "Because in my life, love ends in regret, in suffering. I've brought a lot of my baggage into this partnership. I realize that."

"Self-awareness is meaningless if you don't choose to be better, to do better," he said softly.

"I'm working on this, even if it doesn't always seem that way. Been working on it for years."

He really had no idea how much I'd worked on this. I just hadn't had much success.

We were cumulative, the sum of all of our parts. We were past and present. When Grant and I decided to make room for one another, we made room for all that we carried too. I knew the size and shape of the bags I tugged along and when they were placed at his feet, he had to decide if he was able to sustain the additional weight. And it was a lot of weight.

We learned each other slowly, and I liked him, even with all of the things he carried. Grant had baggage too. He was raised in Prince George's County, Maryland. He was an only child, so he received twice the love for a long time. "We were the American dream. My parents were perfect," he whispered one night, as we lay in his bed, illuminated by moonlight and streetlights. "...Until they weren't."

His mother was diagnosed with cancer when he was nine. "She recovered but my family grew ill and it was incurable. It was like the cancer left her body and attacked all of us instead."

His father had an affair when she went into remission, causing his mother to leave shortly after.

"Did you go with her?"

"No – she left both of us. I saw her on the weekends and spent a few holidays with her, but I was angry for so long that our relationship suffered."

His father battled alcoholism for years; it was his numbing mechanism, Grant called it. "Watching my dad drink until he pissed on himself and having to clean him up – that was high school for me. College was my escape."

He ran his finger along my arm before he sighed and shut his eyes. "Your father's death hit me hard because I haven't spoken to mine in more than a year."

My father.

I sat up on my elbow and ran my fingers through my hair before I shook my head. "It's scary being an adult and seeing family histories and traumas manifest in how we live and love."

"Are you familiar with attachment theory?"

"Are you about to psychoanalyze me, Grant?"

"Yes." He laughed, before he pulled me closer to him and kissed my forehead.

"You act like you've studied psychology for years."

"Just indulge me for a second," he said, his voice soft, tender. "Based on what you've told me, in your relationship with your dad, he wasn't always present and you yearned for a relationship with him but you were often let down. Often felt small and unworthy of love."

I stared at him blankly and he raised his eyebrows. "I'm going to assume that you agree based on your silence."

"Continue."

"There are theories and some evidence, that a child's relationship with their caregiver can later impact how they relate to their partners in romantic relationships. Because your father was always gone, you learned how to pull away from people to protect yourself – to minimize the distress you feel when they leave."

My eyes welled and I shrugged. "Continue."

"...And now it's manifesting with me. You shut down and pull away because it's safe. Even though it hurts you – the potential loss of someone that you love – you've learned how to cope. But now you're discovering that it's self-destructive. I'd hate to watch you implode."

I rolled onto my back and looked up at the ceiling. "Am I messed up?" I whispered.

"Many of us are," he said, before he joined me in our view of his ceiling. "But we learn to love regardless. At least we try."

He rolled over onto his side to face me and I faced him. "Goodnight," I said softly. "Thank you."

CHAPTER 19.

At *Pivot,* the carpet muted the click of my heels as I scurried down the hall to my office on Monday. The metro was running behind this morning and I got out of the house late – a burnt bagel and a bad hair day nearly took me out at the top of the week.

I froze dead in my tracks when I noticed a woman sitting in Vaughn's office with he and Abbi. I studied the three of them before Vaughn looked up and noticed me staring. He scrunched up his face and shooed me away. I retreated to my office and pretended to busy myself with work when I heard Vaughn's office door open. I cracked my door as Abbi and the woman were leaving. Vaughn took a sip of his coffee and stepped out into the hall.

"You should stand fully in your nosiness and come out into the hall."

I gripped the door handle and pulled it open. "What was that? An interview?"

"Yes, with a writer at…gah, the name escapes me now. Abbi brought her in."

"*Thick Mag,*" I said.

"Oh, you know her!"

"…Are y'all planning to hire her?"

"I had someone else in mind but I have to consult with Abbi." He raised his eyebrows. I'd expressed interest in the position for months.

I walked back into my office and pushed the door shut when Vaughn stopped the door mid-push and walked in. He shut the door and watched me walk toward the window.

"The hell is up with you? First, I look up and see you staring at the girl through the window on the verge of tears and now you're throwing a tantrum."

"I hate when you do that. Stop reducing my emotionality to a tantrum."

"Then talk! Like an adult!"

He and I got into these disputes often. Despite being my superior, Vaughn and I were friends. When I first arrived in D.C., I was lonely, navigating a world that felt foreign and cold, and he was quick to jump in and assist with my transition.

I owed him the world for that.

"I know her – that woman – because she's Quentin's fiancé."

Vaughn gasped and jumped away from the desk. He was dramatic. "Why didn't you just say that?"

I smacked my lips before I pressed my greasy forehead against the window and shrugged. "Abbi's hiring her for the staff writer position, isn't she?"

"I recommended you," he said.

As if that were any conciliation. I knew a lot about her – the fiancé. I'd stalked her LinkedIn and read her work. All of it. She was good. Damn good! I didn't measure up – at least not now. Not here at *Pivot*.

"Abbi hated my pitch last week," I mumbled, half-hoping to be wrong.

Vaughn plopped down in front of my desk, "Nia, sit."

I sat down at my desk and he studied me, choosing his words carefully.

"I hired you because you were bold and raw, untouched, pure. The world hadn't muted you yet, hadn't dimmed your light," he said. "You have a voice, a perspective that is so necessary, but you are terrified of using it, terrified of claiming the power of your words. You have to transform your silence and set your words free."

"That's what my work is, Vaughn. That's why I'm here. That's why I've always been here, doing this writing shit, even when it hasn't been fruitful. I'm still here."

"I worry that you've spent too much time and energy pursuing validation from others," he said. "The more you seek yourself externally, the more difficult it'll be to focus on the within working outward – on being the writer you're destined to be."

"I'm not quiet," I said to him, suddenly feeling defensive. "I'm a writer." My voice dropped and shook with trepidation. I hadn't convinced Vaughn and I hadn't convinced myself. My confidence in that moment was flimsy at best.

How did I get here?

"You are quiet," he said and a small smile emerged. "I studied your work before I called you and when I found *Brown Girl*, I expected to meet a woman with fire in her eyes."

"Who'd you meet instead?" I asked.

Vaughn's face fell a little.

"A woman looking for her fire in others," he said softly.

I hadn't won the day, or the week for that matter. Abbi hired her. Her name was Alexa and the name rung in my head on a constant loop as I threw darts in the basement of a dive bar in Chinatown. I waited for Grant to arrive while I took a sip of my second beer. He shuffled through the crowd and when he found me, he took off his coat and hung it up next to mine. He kissed my cheek and ordered a drink from the bar before we started a game of pool.

I was solids, he was stripes. His hand gripped the pool stick and he made a shot behind his back. I rolled my eyes and fought a smile.

"Such a show-off," I said.

"I'm trying to impress you."

"Not impressed." I stuck out my tongue playfully and smiled at him through the musk and haziness of the small bar.

He came around and leant up against the table. He busied himself and chalked our pool cues while he asked me about work.

"That's a no-fly zone tonight," I said, before I finished my beer and tossed him a look.

He furrowed his brow. "The promotion..." he said softly, remembering a conversation we had earlier in the week.

I shrugged and sat on the edge of the table, allowing my legs to swing.

"That's the second promotion you haven't been selected for since I've known you."

"Tread lightly, will you?" I asked. Goosebumps emerged on my arms – a useless, evolutionary response to the cool draft in this bar or my fear of this conversation. A conversation I didn't want to have. I held my hands on my arms and ran my warm fingers over the raised skin.

"Why are you staying at *Pivot*?"

I shrugged. "Not sure I'd want to be anywhere else. *Pivot* is everything I'd want a publication to be."

"You sure about that?"

He and I locked eyes and he grabbed my hand. I pulled away from him and hopped off of the table. "C'mon, let's finish," I said.

He ran his tongue over his teeth before he put his stick down. "I need another drink."

When he walked away from the table, I shut my eyes and exhaled. Grant deserved the softer sides of me that I'd locked away, but I struggled with mustering up the courage to show him. That would require me to be vulnerable, and to acknowledge that I needed someone other than myself.

He returned wearing a familiar look of contemplation. I was often the impetus for that. Grant wasn't quick to anger, but I could always tell when I'd frustrated him. I walked toward him and grabbed his hand in the middle of the bar and kissed his cheek. He looked down at our hands and then up at me.

"Your place or mine?" I asked.

Grant smiled and shook his head as he racked the balls. "Your place. And you owe me another game."

***

Alexa was the opposite of me. Through close observation and some consultation with Joyce, I'd come to that conclusion. Quentin handpicked her because she wasn't anything like me. She wore a lot of gray and pink, colors that flattered her fair skin. Her loose, wavy curls hung at her shoulders and her soft voice matched her short, petite stature. I walked into the lounge one afternoon to find her there, preparing her coffee and reading emails on her iPad.

I offered a tight-lipped, toothless smile on the way to the fridge and she looked over her shoulder at me. "Thanks for the succulent. I'm excited to decorate my office," she said.

"Vaughn bought me one when I started," I said softly, as I added almond milk creamer to my coffee. The dark coffee lightened with a few stirs of my spoon and I looked from my mug to Alexa as she studied me.

She hadn't mentioned Quentin and neither had I. Before she started at *Pivot*, we ran into each other at the grocery store once.

Quentin was pushing the cart and she was reading off of a handwritten grocery list. The two of them were buying cereals and I was at the end of the aisle looking for oatmeal. I spotted it when I saw the two of them. Quentin saw me first and we stood staring at each other until Alexa noticed.

"Hi," she said, smiling awkwardly at me.

"Babe this is Nia," he said. "Nia this is Alexa."

I hadn't taken my eyes off of him and hearing *babe* come from his mouth was like a dagger through the heart – or a shank in my side. When I finally came to, I waved a little and pushed past the cart, heading toward the oatmeal. I didn't end up buying any – and I didn't eat oatmeal for at least three months after the encounter.

Alexa's ring shimmered under the fluorescent light in the lounge and when she noticed me staring, she slid her hand into her pocket and smiled a little.

"Anything I should know about surviving this place?"

"Vaughn will kill you if he finds out that you're using his mug."

"Oh is this his?" she asked. Her face flushed red and I smiled and nodded.

"The obnoxious Michigan mug is his. Anything in this office from Michigan belongs to Vaughn. Abbi is more of a coffee and tea type of person around 10:30 so if you wanted to schmooze, you wouldn't find her in here before then. Oh, and the third floor bathroom has really great lighting for selfies."

She smiled and nodded. "Thanks, Nia."

I turned to leave and she called after me. "I know that this isn't ideal – you and I working so closely together – but I'm hopeful that we'll create some really great content."

"Same here," I said softly.

Our department threw a small celebration for Alexa, welcoming her to the team a few weeks after she arrived. I didn't want to stay, but Vaughn convinced me to.

"It would be big of you," he said. "Not just personally, but professionally."

I agreed. I managed to find a comfortable corner with Joyce and a few other colleagues. I had my gripes with the place, but I did enjoy a *Pivot* party. Wine, hors d'oeuvres and a solid playlist kept my annoyance at bay as I made small talk and watched the clock. It was a little after six when I retreated to my office to leave for the evening.

My door cracked and I looked up to see Quentin standing there with a beer in his hand. My heart betrayed me and fluttered a little in my chest as he cracked a smile and walked into the office. The fluttering was a reflexive response – or one that had been conditioned. My head and heart were suddenly out of sync, as my head was less than pleased to see him.

"Vaughn told me you were on your way out so I wanted to catch you."

I sat my bag down on my desk and studied him. "Alexa know you're in here bothering me?" I smiled a little to lighten the mood. He stood near the door as we attempted to navigate the distance and time between us.

"She does." He smirked, before he took a swig of the beer and looked around the office. "This is nice. It fits you."

I shrugged a little and looked down at my toes – I was in the middle of changing my shoes when he walked in. "It's alright," I said. "How are things at the *Washington Daily?*"

"You've been keeping up with me?" he asked, as he walked toward the line of cards and balloons I hadn't thrown away. He kneeled down and picked up one of the cards before he ran his finger over the front – a soft pink and blue print with *My Condolences* scripted in gold.

"Work is good. How are you?" he asked.

"I'm fine," I said. He looked up at me before he stood up and walked toward my desk. He sat the beer down and slid his hands into his pockets.

"No really, how are you?" he asked.

I raised my eyebrows before I folded my arms. "Quentin, I'm fine."

He shook his head and looked at the corner of gifts. "You haven't gotten rid of the cards and a few of your plants are dying," he said softly, as he walked toward the peace lilies I kept in the corner – an office gift from my mother when I graduated from my cubicle. His brief scan of the room was less of a sign of his curiosity and more of an evaluation of my emotional state.

"Have you considered going back to therapy?"

"Quentin, please."

"Something is going on with you. Eight years later and you still think you can lie to me when you're in pain."

"Well I think we've both overestimated how well we know each other."

Quentin steadied his gaze and clenched his jaw tight before he resumed his drinking with another swig of his beer. I took in the sight of him. I hadn't seen him since that day in the grocery store. Before that, I hadn't seen him since the day he moved out of our apartment.

When I got to D.C. after graduation from Monroe, we messed around until I asked him to be with me for the long haul. "For real this time," I said, as I tousled his hair and marveled at the way it felt between my fingers. "For real this time," he repeated, before he kissed me.

Our pace was too quick and the move was premature. We hadn't resolved any of our issues and we'd given time the responsibility of making us better humans. I was still stubborn in my willingness to let him in fully and he grew to resent me for it. Midday calls became less frequent and his days at work grew longer. Arrivals at home were later. Cologne was new and soon his haircut was different. Sex with him felt distant and we didn't cuddle after anymore.

"Are you happy with me?" I asked one afternoon. We were sitting on the couch with each other, watching another insufferable re-run of *Law & Order*. Our living room was never tidy – the coffee table overrun with books and newspapers. The home of journalists. Quentin glanced at me before his eyes watered. I grabbed his hands and cradled them in my lap. He looked away from me before he shook his head.

"Not anymore Nia," he whispered.

I let go of his hands and grabbed his empty glass. "Want some more beer?" I asked, before I stood up and headed toward the kitchen. I didn't want to acknowledge what I already knew – that he and I were over.

"I've been seeing someone else," he said.

His voice was low, cowardly. I froze for a moment before I turned and threw the glass against the wall. He jumped and his eyes grew wide with terror. "Nia, what the hell?"

I looked down at the mess I'd made before I scurried to the kitchen and grabbed the broom and dustpan. "Sorry," I whispered. "I'm sorry."

In a matter of moments, my world shattered like that glass. But I didn't have a dustpan that was big enough to clean up the mess. He moved out of the apartment a few days later and I cried in the corner of our bedroom, clutching a bottle of whiskey Vaughn recommended. I developed a love for Maker's during the break-up – we were great friends to one another. After he left, he sent me a few emails when I blocked his phone number. I still refused to see him.

Now, a stranger stood in the middle of my office willing me to open up to him. A man who thought that he knew me. A man who didn't know me at all anymore. "We once knew each other better than anyone else," he managed to say finally.

I shook my head and put my bag on my shoulder. "I don't know you Quentin. Not anymore," I said softly. "And no, I'm not alright. But I will be."

Alexa appeared. She lightly tapped the door with her middle knuckle. "Are you ready?" she asked.

Quentin shifted his eyes from me to her and she gave the two of us a look – one that was not assumptive. She didn't look threatened, for I wasn't a threat. Not anymore.

I was a season that passed some time ago.

CHAPTER 20.

My first trip to the gynecologist was after the rape. I was afraid that I was pregnant when my period was late the following month. I told my mother that my menstrual cramps were more painful than usual and she made an appointment to see a nurse practitioner in the same office as her gynecologist. At the appointment, I urged my mother to stay in the waiting room and we bickered for a while until she let me go alone.

I put my feet in the stirrups and stared up at the overhead light. The nurse pushed my legs apart and told me to relax. I shut my eyes tight as she tore through any ounce of innocence I had left. The speculum was cold, the feeling foreign, and the pinch unbearable. *I screamed!* I gasped, I cried out for my mother. I wanted her there and nowhere near me at the same time.

The nurse finished the exam in haste, and when it was all over, my scream rung in my ears as I lay lifeless with my legs shut tight. My thighs trembled long after she'd removed the speculum. She turned off the light and studied me.

"Nia, have you experienced any recent sexual trauma? Rapes or molestations?" she asked.

"Why?" I asked, wiping away tears and sitting up.

"Your response to my exam," she said softly. "I used the smallest speculum I have."

I looked toward the door. "Are you going to tell my mother?"

"You're eighteen. I won't, but I think that you should. Have you reported the incident?"

"No," I said. "I just need to know if I'm pregnant."

She explained that she was also going to check for sexually transmitted infections. "I don't have an STI," I said defensively. "I don't have any symptoms."

"Some infections are asymptomatic – there aren't always signs that you can see or feel. Sometimes damage is being done internally and we aren't aware."

I didn't have an STI and I wasn't pregnant, but I realized years later when I walked into Dr. Johnson's office that I'd been battling an infection of the mind and spirit since the rape, and it had been asymptomatic for many years. Its latency was not less destructive, for the trauma was like a sleeping giant, waiting to be stirred awake.

My experience of grief felt asymptomatic most days. There wasn't a burn or dull ache to signal the need for healing. Grief for me looked like work until 7:30 every night. Grief was gym and jogs with Grant on Saturday afternoons. Grief was crying in the shower and feeling ashamed about crying.

Grief was pushing through.

Grief was living.

I went to my mailbox after work one evening to find one lonely letter. While I waited for the elevator, I studied the envelope – there was no return address. I waited until I got into my apartment to read it. There was a worn yellow piece of paper, ripped from a writing pad with a piece of beautiful stationary stapled to the front. I scanned it quickly and plopped down in the middle of the floor.

My sister finally cleaned out our father's apartment and found a letter he'd written to me shortly before his death. I took a few deep breaths before I walked to my minibar and poured myself a glass of red wine. I took two big gulps before I looked back at the yellow sheet of paper sitting on the coffee table.

I didn't want to read it, but I knew that I had to. I finished my glass of wine and gripped the tattered sheet. I studied his handwriting – I hadn't seen it since I was younger. I put the sheet to my nose, wondering if he'd left a scent behind.

To my daughter Nia,

When I last saw you, you were fifteen. You wore shorts and a green tank top. I remember looking at you and seeing your mother and me all at once. You were beautiful and brown. My baby girl, standing in young womanhood with so much grace.

I apologize for all of the pain that I've caused, for the questions I've left you with, for the nights at the dinner table alone with your mother. I apologize for the empty seat at your dance recitals, and your high school and college graduations. I apologize for never being there when I promised that I would be.

There is so much that I could say to you – so much that I'll never get the chance to say to you. My beautiful, brown, baby girl, please know that I think about you everyday. I've let years and my pride get in the way, and now it is much too late. I hope that this letter finds you some day. It can't bring back the years I've missed, but it is my final goodbye. Happy birthday, Sweet Pea. I love you.

Daddy

I ruptured. This was not closure and it was no conciliation. I'd been in denial. For months, his death trailed behind me like it was my shadow, dark and silent. I tried to move on. I boxed up my grief and shoved it to the back of mind. I dealt with it by walking around it, stacking things on top of it, but never lifting it – never opening it or reckoning with its contents. I lied on the couch and read the letter three more times, before I ripped it up and burned it over the kitchen sink.

Weeks passed and I thought about him when I didn't want to – in the morning while I was putting on my make-up, at night when I wrote in my journal. I thought about closure and what it must feel like. I thought about how far away I was from that.

My sister called a few weeks later. I was finishing up at work when her name popped up on my phone. I answered quickly while I gathered my things, hoping to get out of the office. I wanted to leave before Vaughn found something else for me to do.

"Nia, it's Natalie."

"Hi, how are you?" I asked dismissively, while I scanned my desk for the jump drive I'd need to take home with me.

"Not too good, I'm afraid to say."

I paused. "Is everything alright?"

"So I've been on a long, arduous journey this past year with my health. A lot of blood work and tests. I was finally diagnosed this afternoon – I have lupus, like our father."

I sat down on the floor and allowed the contents of my bag to spill out on the carpet. "I'm sorry, Natalie. I can't imagine what you must be going through. Do you have some people to look after you?"

"I do. I'm blessed. Folks have been with me the entire time. I called you because I think you should go to the doctor. Our father died from kidney failure – a complication of his lupus. I want you to be sure that you're in the clear."

I froze, my mouth slightly ajar. She continued to talk but I didn't hear her – couldn't hear her. Lupus? Was I *sick*? "I don't have anything. I'm fine," I said, shaking my head feverishly.

"There aren't always symptoms. Lupus can look different from one person to the next. I didn't call to diagnose you – just wanted to let you know that I'm thinking about you. I hope that you're well. I really do."

Autoimmune Disease, Lupus, Systemic Lupus Erythematosus. I sat on the floor of my office with Google and WebMD in front of me for a few hours. I read up as much as I could until I decided to make an appointment with my doctor.

It won't hurt to get some blood work done, I thought.

***

Genetic markers. Antinuclear Antibody Test. Rheumatologist. My primary care physician handed me a packet describing the ANA test, and what a positive or negative screening meant for me. I struggled to remember any of the details – I was terrified.

I had to get blood drawn and leave a urine sample. In the lab, I watched the nurse poke around for a vein to draw blood. I shut my eyes and looked away from the needle. "You're going to feel a little pinch." My eyes watered and I bit my lip. I'd hated needles and shots since I was a child.

They shoved a small cup in my hand and gave me instructions for the urine sample before I was free to go. I stayed in the bathroom longer than I needed to and cried. When I was done, I walked out into the waiting room to find Grant sitting there. I saw him before he saw me. I hadn't ever seen him look so nervous. He held my workbag and coat with a tight grip while he waited for me to come out.

When he saw me approach, he fixed his face and smiled warmly. "How'd it go?" He tried to be brave for me and I was thankful for that.

We walked outside and ate lunch together before we were both due back at work. He rubbed my thigh and studied my face. "Don't claim anything yet," he said. My mother said the same, and Cecilia too.

I was optimistic but I was afraid. I'd finally started to deal with the emotional brokenness and damage done by my father, but I hadn't considered the possibility of inheriting physical brokenness from him. Grant kissed me goodbye and I watched him drive away. I worried that this might be too much for him, that all of this would remind him of hard times with his mother.

I didn't go to work that day – I called out and lied on my living room floor instead. I finished another jar of peanut butter and listened to Miles Davis for hours. When I finally had the strength to pull myself together, I decided to write. The anger, grief, confusion were my fuel – I had to push forward.

After his death, my father left behind more questions than answers, but I wanted to free myself of the desire to find them. It was an unhealthy burden – he'd been an unhealthy burden for so long. I let my mind loose and I wrote to him. Wherever he was, I hoped he'd receive my words.

The Father Daughter Dance
Nia Landrey

For most of my life, you drove a 1997 Ford Escort. It was gray with rusted door hinges, holes in the seat and a broken cassette player. I remember running my hands along the dashboard, picking up dust and crumbs along the way. I'd wipe my hands on the tattered seats. I remember the sound of your car horn and the rusted engine when you would enter the driveway. I'd hand you tools from the toolbox while you worked on the car for hours. It was the only thing I'd ever seen you work hard to maintain.

I still remember my mother's face in the window – her waving goodbye or rushing out of the house to snatch me from the backseat. Oh, and I remember the seatbelt because it would always get jammed. She'd yell at you about that, before she'd carry me toward the door. You would drive off into the night and I'd wait by the window until the next visit.

Until there weren't more visits; until weeklong lapses became months and then years. Until I didn't remember the sound of your voice, just the sound of the car horn and the rusted engine. For Father's Day one year, I made you a card and drew a brand new sports car. I couldn't buy you one, but I hoped that a picture would suffice. You'd missed the first Father Daughter Dance that year, but I was young and hopeful that you'd be at the next. Until you didn't make the next, or the one after that. Until I stopped expecting you to be there for anything.

At school, they put me in a counseling group for brown girls without daddies. A group for girls raised by single mothers. In my white, suburban school, they placed six chairs in a circle and asked five brown girls to talk about their experience of "daddylessness." I didn't speak for four months, and my counselor recommended therapy to work through my abandonment issues. Funny, I hadn't felt abandoned until I knew that there was a word for it.

An abandoned girl grows into an adult with attachment issues; an adult who cradles love in an open palm, for she understands that holding on too tight will leave callouses. She's had enough callouses, enough wounds that have healed with thickened skin. She's got thick skin and

thick ego, but she's fragile. Prone to breakage. You cared more about a rusted engine than the rusted girl you left standing alone at the Father Daughter Dance. She's deteriorating, too.
And now it is much too late to dance.

CHAPTER 21.

I pondered my own mortality after my doctor's appointment. I thought about what death was and what it wasn't. I considered a life that wasn't the life I thought I'd live. And I thought about love. I thought about loving and living constantly. Mostly, I thought about the absence of those things. No more life. No more love.

The future felt uncertain. Everything was more time-sensitive – especially loving and living. I had to pursue my purpose in light of these revelations, for life was finite. I wrote at least twenty pitches before I finally settled on one – I wanted to write about death.

Vaughn raised his eyebrows. "What?"

"Just go with me," I said, before I sat down across from him and handed him what I'd written – the piece about my father.

"I want to interview women – black women – about grief and loss, encountering death and choosing life."

Vaughn's window was cracked, inviting city noises and chirping birds into his office. He toyed with a fidget spinner before he sat back in his seat and studied me over his glasses. He took them off and shook his head. "It needs to be rooted in something. I need an issue, a challenge. What are you seeking to tackle?"

"Healing," I said softly.

He nodded. "I get the sense that you are seeking to heal through your own story and through the stories of other women, but in order for the pitch to be successful with Abbi, you have to give her something to bite."

"…Mental health disparities in the black community."

His lips rose into a smile and he nodded. "That's something we can eat. I'll set up a meeting with Abbi."

I was finally excited about something, albeit not quite the story I wanted to pitch, but I was close. These were the narratives I wanted to explore, the stories I missed telling for *Brown Girl.* When it was finally time for my meeting with Abbi, she listened to the entire pitch this time.

She squinted her eyes and pursed her lips before she nodded – a condescending nod, I could feel it. "Mmm. This is coming from a real place and I value that," she said softly.

She promised to get back to me in a few days. I half-believed her, but hoped for the best. I believed in this story. I believed in me.

Days passed without a response from Abbi and my confidence shrank to the size of a pea. I sat behind my desk one evening with my shoes off and the space heater on. I had a few stories that I needed to edit by midnight.

"I ordered you some Chinese food. It's on the way to your office," Grant said on the phone, as I took my laptop to the floor and poured myself some of the wine I had stashed in my desk.

"I'm sorry for canceling on you again this week. I'm not avoiding you," I said.

"I'll see you this weekend. You can bring your work over," he said.

Grant was patience personified and I was grateful. I smiled on my end of the phone and nodded. "See you soon. I'd like some spring rolls, too."

"I already ordered them," he said.

The door to my office opened and Alexa popped her head in. "Hey, do you have a minute or two?"

I nodded and sat up. I put my wine glass behind me and studied the manila envelope she pulled out of her bag. "So Abbi shared your pitch with me."

I parted my lips to object – Abbi was the editor, not Alexa. My mind raced as I forced a smile and nodded. *What the hell?*

"What'd you think?" I asked.

She pushed her hair behind her ear. "I think it's…an incredibly brave venture. You're tackling your complicated relationship with your father in a way that feels very genuine. Your transparency was not lost on us."

Us? She's speaking for Abbi, too?

I sat up against the desk and pushed my lips to the side. "Dumping the pitch, huh?"

"Not dumping!" she said, before she smiled. "Just tabling it for now. We want to rework this a little bit. There is a lot that we could do with this."

She put the envelope on my desk and stood awkwardly near the door when she noticed my glass of wine. "Staying late tonight?"

"More edits," I said before I took a sip of the wine and shrugged.

"Keep pushing. You're a great writer, Nia."

I looked up at her. From where she stood, the lamp in the room cast shadows across her face, while I sat fully bathed in light, fully exposed. I nodded. "Thanks, Alexa."

She left the office and I stared at the spot where she stood a few moments earlier before I grabbed my phone and called Vaughn.

"Don't approach Abbi with this," he warned.

"Well what am I supposed to do? Never pitch a story? I feel like I hung myself out there to dry, Vaughn. Who knows if she even read it?"

"She read it and then she probably consulted with Alexa."

"Why though? Why wouldn't she consult with you?"

Vaughn was quiet for a moment before he sighed. "Look, you didn't hear this from me. Abbi is concerned that Alexa's work is a little stiff. It's not very relatable and she's concerned that our readers won't respond well to her. It's possible that Abbi shared your story with her as an example of what she could produce if she were more sincere."

"Wait, let me get this straight…"

"Nia…"

"No, because this is crazy, Vaughn. Why would Abbi use my work as an example for Alexa? Could've promoted my ass instead!"

"I need you to let that go, sis."

"And I need you to understand why I feel slighted by Abbi."

"I do understand."

"Why didn't I get the job? I'm sure Abbi told you."

"…She didn't think that you were polished enough."

"BULL! I could've become more polished, but you can't teach sincerity."

"You're right."

He and I were quiet on the phone for a while before he sighed. "If it were up to me, you would've gotten the job. Something is going to open up for you soon. Abbi sees how hard you're working."

Hard work didn't pay at *Pivot*, and it hadn't paid off. I took Vaughn's advice and I waited. I didn't address Abbi about my pitch or my future at *Pivot*. I waited in the wings for a breakthrough.

About a month later, when *Pivot's* new issue was done and published, I spent my lunch reviewing it. Our feature story was an interview with a natural hair blogger based in Seattle. I was able to sit in on her interview with Vaughn. She and I spoke for an hour about predominantly white spaces and natural hair. I remember telling her how much I appreciated a predominately black space like *Pivot* – how I felt supported and encouraged. I skimmed the feature and jumped to the next story. I read the title before I furrowed my brow and searched for the author.

Daddy & Me
Alexa Walsh

I read through the story and clutched my stomach, suddenly feeling sick. Alexa lost her father when she was twelve. He died in a car accident and she used religion to pull herself out of the depths of grief. She interviewed women with similar stories and explored how the church plays an integral role in grief management for African Americans. I pushed away my lunch and shut my laptop before I stood up and stormed into Vaughn's office. I slammed his door and he jumped.

"Another tantrum?"

When he saw my face, he slowly shut his computer and sighed. "Nia…"

"Don't," I said as I walked across the office and sat down on the couch. I could barely articulate my thoughts. I was so furious. "…That was basically my story. My pitch," I said.

"A derivative of your idea, sure," Vaughn said.

I gave him a side eye and he joined me on the couch in his office. I shut my eyes and sighed. "It took me months to write about my father," I said softly. "I allowed y'all into my cracks, Vaughn. I built a pitch that was *so* deeply personal to me. I feel betrayed."

He apologized and I smiled a little and shook my head.

"Where were you in all of this? Alexa's story must've crossed your desk," I said.

"I didn't see it until this morning. Abbi must've slipped it in after I gave my final edits."

I wrote with my soul. That pitch meant more to me than Alexa or Abbi cared to know. In the middle of another half-cooked apology, I stood up to leave Vaughn's office.

"Nia, it won't be the last time."

I stopped and turned to look at him. "What?" I asked.

"It's the nature of the beast," he said, before he stood up and put his hands in his pockets. "Keep your pitches close and your enemies closer. Protect your ideas but know that as soon as you share them, they're no longer yours. You can't copyright an idea."

The lamp in Vaughn's office cast shadows across his face but bathed me in light, like with Alexa the other night. The congruence was apparent – I had to stay in the light.

When I left his office, I listened to a voicemail left by my doctor's office. My results were in. I needed to come in for an appointment.

CHAPTER 22.

I called my mother from the floor of my living room, trying to swallow what I could from my dry mouth. My vocal chords shook and my stomach flipped. I had to schedule a follow-up with the doctor, and my mother was on a flight to D.C. less than twelve hours later.

She slept on my overpriced couch and she didn't complain when I joined her in the middle of the night. Despite my longer limbs and the physical distance I'd put between us for years now, I craved nothing more than to be closer to her, cramped on a couch.

At the appointment, she held my hand while we waited. She quizzed me on song lyrics – a favorite pastime of ours and I remembered how much I loved her.

"That's an easy one – Rachelle Ferrell, "With Open Arms." You played that like every morning that summer I had a cast on. My eyes are crossing at the thought," I said.

"You secretly loved Rachelle," she said.

"I still do."

When my primary care doctor walked into the room, I couldn't tell if she was bringing good news or bad news. She was always stoic. My mother offered me a smile and squeezed my hand. The doctor sat down and took off her glasses.

"The ANA test came back positive."

My heart cracked in half and my mother squeezed a little tighter. "What does that mean?" she asked. The words jumped out of her before I'd even thought to ask.

"We can't diagnose her just yet," the doctor said.

I had to see a specialist. I needed to be monitored for a year or two. My mind was cloudy; thoughts swirled around and I waded through them all like I was waist-deep in murky water. I couldn't see the bottom, couldn't feel the bottom.

As my mother bombarded her with questions, I bit my lip and grabbed my purse quietly. "Nia don't you have any questions?" my mother asked.

"Which rheumatologist would you like me to see?" I asked.

She left the referral with the front desk and I locked myself in a bathroom stall and avoided processing for a while. I made dinner plans with Grant and scheduled an appointment for a pedicure. My mother waited outside for twenty-five minutes before she walked into the bathroom and found my stall. "You can't run from this, Sweet Pea."

"I'm not running," I said softly. I unlocked the stall and she walked in to join me. She cupped my face with her hands and kissed my forehead.

"You'll be fine."

"What if I'm not?" I challenged. My eyes welled. "I'm scared, Ma."

"Me too," she said, before she nodded and looked me in the eye. "This will not break you, but you may have to bend a little," she whispered. "We're going to get through this."

***

I set aside my woes for a little while and went to Grant's apartment for dinner. He and I sat across from each other at the dining room table, with our plates full of food and work. We were both behind and had deadlines to meet.

"Vaughn said what?" Grant asked, looking up from his stack of ungraded essays. My digital to-do pile matched his. I had a number of interview transcriptions to work on for Vaughn and Alexa.

"He said that this wouldn't be the last time one of my ideas would be stolen."

Grant licked his fingers before he turned to another page of the essay he was reading. He shook his head and marked it up quickly. With five years in the classroom under his belt, he could review a three-page assignment with record speed and leave individual comments.

"I don't get it. Isn't there some ethical obligation for writers and journalists?" he asked.

"Well I was always taught to expect that editors would act ethically. Pitches and ideas get stolen, sure, but not at a place like *Pivot*. Vaughn has always shown integrity in his work and has expected that of everyone else."

"Until now?" Grant asked, before he took a sip of his drink – a "ho-jito" he called it. "Has Vaughn checked Abbi?"

When I quietly returned to transcribing, Grant took another sip of his drink and nodded, understanding what my silence meant. "So when are you resigning?"

"I'm not resigning," I said, before I laughed. "I just have to be more careful."

"Or you could find a place where you and your ideas are safe."

"That doesn't exist anywhere."

"It would if you had your own publication."

I rolled my eyes and blew air through my teeth. "That's a dream I sold long ago."

"Sold or traded in for a 401k and an apartment on Florida Avenue?"

"Self-publishing doesn't pay."

"Not immediately but it will. You're mad talented. I get it – you need something steady until you get the ball rolling."

"Yes, and *Pivot* will have to be that in the meantime."

"Are you happy there?"

I looked over at him and shrugged before he stood up and walked to the white board he had in the living room. He used it for practically everything: his grocery list, a spending budget for the month and drink recipes he wanted to try.

He wiped the board clean and wrote "Values" before he drew a line underneath. "Is this how you run your classroom?" I asked, smiling in amusement.

"You wouldn't be in my classroom with that low-cut shirt." He chuckled before he turned and studied me curiously. "What do you value most about writing?"

"I don't know."

"I won't accept that. You do know."

"So this *is* how you run your classroom."

"Nia, do this with me. Please."

I let my grin fade before I thought through the answer. "Writing can heal. Writing preserves moments I may lose or forget otherwise. Writing shapes the way that I think. Writing allows others into my world. Writing shapes the way that others think about my world."

He was busy writing notes before he circled the key words: heal, preserve, shape. He stood back and tapped his chin with the expo marker before he smiled a little and looked over at me.

"Have you thought about teaching?"

I fell out into laughter and grabbed his ho-jito before I took a sip and glanced at him. "Are you serious right now?"

"I'm holding an expo marker. I'm definitely serious right now."

"Where are you going with this?"

"Indulge me for a second." One of his favorite phrases. "My school just got this huge grant for after school programming and they're looking for activities for our students. What if you taught a creative writing class?"

"Where did you get creative writing class from what I just told you?" I asked.

"Well, at the heart of what you value about writing is healing, preservation and shaping narratives. Writing doesn't have to happen at a magazine. It can happen in schools, in classrooms, with students."

"Grant I don't teach. I'm not a teacher."

"You aren't necessarily coming to teach. You're coming to heal. Teaching is the medium but healing is the goal."

I stared at the white board for a while before he came and kissed my forehead. "Let me know. No pressure – just an idea."

He ran his hands through my hair and allowed his fingers to get caught on the kinks and coils. "I'm interested," I said softly.

He resumed his seat at the table and I studied him. He glanced at me and winked and I felt my heart swell in my chest, almost like it was making more room for him.

"How was your doctor's appointment today?" he asked, as he turned to a new essay.

I nodded and forced a smile. "Nothing to report."

CHAPTER 23.

Grant was a high school English teacher at a charter school in Southeast, D.C. I hadn't been to Southeast much since my move to D.C., but I'd heard about the areas east of the Anacostia River at work and on the news. Southeast was predominantly black with a rich history, and the community was fighting to preserve that history in the face of "renewal."

A few of the writers at *Pivot* were buying property and looking at houses *east of the river*. Even without a full understanding of D.C.'s geography, I knew that this interest in real estate in Southeast signified a phenomenon I'd grown familiar with during my time in the District – the big G. Gentrification was a buzzword in some spaces, a swear word in others. It was caustic – almost acidic on the tongue. When I drove to Grant's school one afternoon, I finally had the chance to see tangible evidence of the big G, as I drove in and out of the targeted investment I'd heard so much about.

Grant worked for a high-performing school that was part of a national charter network. He met me on the steps of the large school. They'd recently moved into a new building after being housed in a church for two years. He beamed with joy as he gave me a tour of the space. A few students stopped him in the hall. Some were bold enough to ask him if I was his girlfriend, to which he blushed and shooed them away to class.

"Most of them think I live alone with a dog in Maryland," he said.

"You don't even like dogs," I laughed.

"It doesn't matter when they've got their minds made up."

We went into the library and he showed me the space that could potentially be mine for the creative writing class if I wanted it. I walked around the room and studied the shiny new computer monitors. I looked at him and nodded.

"I like it a lot."

"So what do you think? My principal is excited about the proposal you sent over. It wouldn't be a lot of money but it'd be something for your time."

I paused for a moment before a student stuck her head into the room. "Mr. Carter?"

Grant nodded at the student and stuck out his hand. She handed him a composition notebook and turned to leave before he stopped her. "Riley, come meet Ms. Nia."

She walked into the room, revealing the baby bump her twig-like legs managed to carry. She waddled a little toward me and adjusted her bag on her shoulder. "Hi, I'm Riley."

I shook her hand and smiled. "Ms. Nia writes for *Pivot*, an online magazine. She'll be teaching a creative writing class after school starting next week," Grant said.

Riley's eyes lit up. "Did you study English?" she asked quickly.

"Journalism," I said, as I leant up against a table in the room. "Are you a writer?"

"I want to be," she said.

She already was. Grant shared some of the writing in her composition book after she left. He and I sat in the library long after the students were gone for the day. I leant back in my chair and looked around, my mind in a million places. Riley's writing was raw, full of content I wasn't sure I could address. I'd finally gotten to a place in my life where I could begin to contend with my own trauma. How on earth could I help someone else through theirs?

***

I spent more than four hours Sunday night doing a flexi-rod set on my hair. My coils rebelled like they often did, unyielding and unwilling to do anything but curl on their own time. I stared at the wet, puffy mess I'd made and shoved it up into a bun before I scurried out of the door to get to work by 6:30.

After my pitch was stolen, I moved some mental furniture around and made room for a new strategy. I worked longer hours, taught the class at Grant's school and took on some freelancing gigs to make some money – enough money to leave *Pivot*.

I walked into my office to find three hot-pink sticky notes on my keyboard – a sign that Alexa had been there the night before. I read each of them before I crumpled them in my palm and tossed them into the trashcan. I completed the shortest tasks first, answered emails and updated Vaughn and Abbi's calendars before 8:00. When Vaughn got to work and found me there before him for the third week in a row, he knocked on my door and raised his eyebrows.

"Early bird gets the worm?" he asked.

I nodded. I hadn't told him about the writing class and I hadn't shared my plan to leave either. I complied with requests without complaint and quietly tucked away my hopes for something bigger. The time to leave would reveal itself soon.

"Just trying to get a few more hours in," I said casually.

I worked through my lunch break, avoided conversations in the lounge and stayed tucked away in my office until it was time to leave. Vaughn watched me scurry around before he came into my office just as I was packing up to leave one evening.

"Hey, one short request," he said.

"What's up? I've got to go."

"Do you? I really need some edits before 6."

"I have a thing after work now," I said to him, as I searched frantically for my manila folder with all of the copies of my lesson plans.

Vaughn held it up. "You left this on the copier."

"Oh!" I shrieked, before I took it from him and put it in my purse.

"Why didn't you tell me you were teaching?"

"I don't know. We haven't really spoken since the whole pitch thing." I jumped out of my heels and slipped into my tennis shoes before he and I met eyes. He frowned a little and nodded.

"Well I think we should talk. Soon." He walked out of my office and I blew air out of my mouth before I scurried outside to catch an Uber. I'd missed the train I needed to catch and if I was more than a few minutes late, the kids would leave and I wouldn't hear the end of it. I scurried into the library seven minutes after four o'clock and my students all craned their necks to look at me. Roland tapped his pencil on the edge of the desk. "Tsk tsk, Ms. Nia. She's late again."

I saw two of them swap dollar bills and I rolled my eyes and laughed a little. "I'm coming from the other side of town. Cut me some slack."

"Nobody told you to work uptown with the white folks," Charidee said, before she popped her gum. She approached me at my desk and studied my outfit before she looked down into my workbag. She spotted a bag of trail mix and smiled. "Your hair looks cute today."

"Compliments do not earn you my snacks! I've told you this."

"But you always give them to me anyway so I might as well try."

She walked to her desk and I settled in with a light smile. After running ragged at *Pivot* all day, I felt like I could breathe here. I went to the board and wrote down a quote while I charged Riley with taking attendance.

Until the lion learns to write, every story will glorify the hunter.
African Proverb

I stood back with my marker before I turned to the class and watched them all process it. The class started with ten students, but we had fifteen more on the waitlist. When word got around that the class would be available this summer, the list of interested students continued to grow. Roland was the first to write down the quote. Grant and I got each of them individual notebooks with their initials inscribed and Roland's was almost full.

Riley raised her hand. "This quote reminds me of our discussion from the first class."

I affirmed her with a smile as Isaiah nodded and pointed at Riley. "I thought the same thing. There's power in the story."

"I think there's power in the story, but there's also power in learning how to tell the story – in being the storyteller," Roland added.

Impressed, I sat atop my desk and opened my trail mix. They continued to bat around ideas until Charidee turned to me.

"What's our prompt today?" she asked.

"As always, I want you to write what you feel led to write but I want us to consider the proverb. In my experience, learning to tell my own story has been incredibly empowering like Roland offered."

"We've talked a lot about your experiences in your neighborhoods. You've seen violence and love coexist in a way that is both jarring and inspiring. But there's another story being told about

Southeast – a story that isn't the full truth. I want you to write the counter-narrative – write the story that glorifies the lion, not the hunter."

Roland's face twisted up – he was a thinker and a planner. Sometimes he'd think for half the class and write an amazing poem in the last twenty minutes. Riley went to work first – she always listed her ideas, before she'd tackle the ones she liked the most. Charidee got up and went to sit in the corner. Isaiah put on his headphones.

I walked around, touching each of their shoulders and reading over what they'd started. At the end of class, I left them with some words, before we said our goodbyes. I bid each of them adieu with a hug and a fruit cup for the commute home. Each night, when I stacked chairs on top of desks and shut down the computers, I took note of the fullness I felt. Like maybe I was finally stepping into my purpose.

***

Grant helped me detangle my hair that evening after I'd left it in a bun for more than a week. The knots he and I fought to get out signified that I hadn't been taking care of my strands. Since the doctor's appointment, I'd been a little preoccupied and my tangled thoughts manifested in the stubborn knots Grant tried to undo.

"Use some of the conditioner," I chuckled.

"I don't know how you do this love," he said before he looked toward the TV. Ohio State was playing Michigan State, and the two were tied in the fourth quarter.

"How was class today?" he asked.

I smiled and nodded my head. "I think I want to publish their work."

"I hope you aren't considering pitching this to *Pivot*," he said.

"Nope," I said. I was ready to lead my own publication again. The brief emotional hiatus at work cleared enough mental space for me to see what I truly desired – a platform to tell stories that mattered to me. It was what I'd sought since I was eighteen.

"I'm starting a submissions-based platform for emerging writers. The mission will be to heal, preserve, and shape the world through stories."

Grant paused his detangling and smirked. "I'm proud of you," he said softly.

We settled into our comfortable silence before I looked down at my hands. "...The ANA test came back positive. I'm sorry I didn't tell you sooner."

Grant sat the comb down and joined me on the floor. He wrapped his arms around me and I cried on his shoulder. It was the first time I'd cried since the appointment. He didn't ask any questions and he didn't pull away. He hardened like the support beam I needed him to be and he held me until I heard the buzzer sound. Ohio State won by three.

CHAPTER 24.

"How have you encountered death?" I asked one afternoon. The library was sweltering – a sign that summer was near. The air conditioning hadn't been working all week. A small box fan pushed around hot air and the kids crowded around, hoping to catch a bit of its breeze.

Roland fanned his face. "This heat feel like death."

"And smell like Roland's breath," Charidee said before she smiled.

"Let's begin," I said softly.

Isaiah raised his hand slowly. "If I don't know shit else, I feel like I know death. From seeing my grandpop pass on in the living room to candlelight vigils in elementary school."

I nodded. Roland's face fell into a more somber hue and he shrugged. "Saw a dude laid out when I was in sixth grade. Just dead behind my apartment building."

"So you've encountered death – most of you. How have you dealt with it?" I asked.

"I don't," Charidee said.

"Too much to bear?" I asked.

"Nah we already bear it. I just don't have the space to process I guess," Charidee said.

"I pray," Riley said, suddenly springing from the quiet she'd nestled under in our last few classes.

"What do you pray for?" I asked her.

She ran her hand over her stomach, traced its circumference. "For something better for my son."

"I want us to begin writing about death today, but I want you to focus on life after death. What does it look like? What does it feel like? I want you to begin processing, Charidee."

Charidee looked up at me and put her hood on before she dropped her head and started writing. We were finalizing pieces to be published, and the students wanted to address topics that felt meaningful to them and their community. Death came up the most in our conversations.

I made them leave their journals behind for me to review. I wanted us to publish and perform before the end of the school year, so the editing and selection process needed to begin. In the evenings, I'd sit in my living room with the journals open on the floor. I turned from one to another, reading beautiful and devastating encounters of death, life and resilience.

Charidee wrote about the carryout at the end of her street. She'd frequented the small, corner restaurant since she was a child. She could barely see over the counter when she'd accompany her grandmother on afternoon walks. There was Crazy Joseph and Big Boy, two neighborhood characters that would sit outside of the carryout singing and drinking. They'd watch out for her and the others for years, until Big Boy got shot and Crazy Joseph passed away. A real estate agent recently approached the owner of the carryout, offering him more money than he'd ever made at the store. He had a choice: to sell or not to sell. Chardiee described how his life would change and how hers would too. The block would die, only to be imbued with a life she wouldn't have access to.

Riley wrote about caskets and bassinets. She was fearful that her baby might need both, like her cousin Jackson. He died in his sleep five months into the life he was supposed to fill. He didn't utter a sound, just died in his crib and joined the angels he often smiled at during naps. Riley could still hear him coo when she'd walk past her cousin's bedroom. Although she wasn't sure if it were a figment of her imagination or the sound of a mother's broken heart beating with irregularity. Either way, she missed him like she missed her unborn child.

Roland described the sound of death. He said it sounded like ambulance sirens in the distance, sounded like the pitter-patter of feet on the pavement after dark. Death sounded like a vodka bottle hitting the dining room table repeatedly, sounded like a mother's scream, sounded like "Dearly Departed." The sound of death was so loud, so ubiquitous, that he hadn't heard much of anything… until he heard the sound of life. Life was a baby's cry and an ice cream truck wailing past children that smelled like outside. Life sounded like a fire hydrant overflowing in the street, go-go music, and the scratchy sound of Styrofoam boxes stained with mumbo sauce. Life sounded like pen to paper. Life sounded like story.

Isaiah wrote about his t-shirt business. He started it after his friend Terrell was shot in eighth grade. He wanted to make shirts for all of his friends with Terrell's basketball number spray painted on the back. After the funeral, he started getting requests. More shirts, more vigils, more *Rest in Peace* in powder blue script. Business always boomed in the summer, he said. Death was profitable; it made his life at home a little better with more money to go around. He thought about quitting – he had no interest in memorializing death any longer. But he didn't stop... especially after he saw Terrell's mom wearing the shirt he made years after her son's funeral. He thought, *maybe he couldn't help the dead, but he could comfort the living.*

***

The day that I was diagnosed with lupus, my mother and I cried and prayed on the phone together, before I dug up my Nana's old bible. My mother slipped it in one of my moving boxes when I went to Monroe but I'd let it collect dust on bookshelves since. Quite strategically, I'd hid it behind books I already read – *out of sight, out of mind*, I thought. My aversion to religion hadn't helped nor healed me, and when I sought solace in other places – men, work, whiskey – I found that my well eventually ran dry. I wanted water – I needed His reign.

My weak hands cradled the book now, seeking answers I didn't think I could find. For weeks, I mulled over my purpose, my reason for being here still. I asked for guidance. I prayed for peace.

For years, I'd wandered – expecting to hear God's voice call out to me but I hadn't been receptive. When an answer finally emerged, it didn't sound like a voice – didn't sound like anything. Instead, I felt an ineffable weight in my stomach – the weight of truth, of purpose.

And I wrote a resignation letter. I was choosing life.

I expected pushback from Vaughn, but he supported me. I called him before I formally submitted the letter to Abbi. "I understand, and I love you," he'd said. The next day, I found a small note from him on my desk, and when I went home I taped it to my bathroom mirror.

"You are much more than a woman with fire in her eyes. You've become the flame. Your words are incendiary. Be bomb, be explosion. Be everything but quiet. I love you – and I'm proud of you."

Cecilia and I worked on my new website, and I sowed my hopes and dreams in what I thought was fertile soil, finally. My mother used to say, *"What we don't reap, rots."* I was ready for my harvest – I just needed to put in some work.

Despite all that she'd taught me, my mother wasn't inspired by my choice. "What do you mean you're resigning? Do you have something else lined up?"

"Well no. Not a full-time job."

My mother paused for a long while. "Then how can you afford to leave *Pivot*? Do you understand the gravity of that? No benefits, no financial security?"

"I have contingency plans."

"Contingency plans? For when you're broke in a few months?"

"Precisely." I smirked.

Joyce raised her eyebrows and took a sip of her tea while she watched me attempt to defend my choice. "I'm out with Joyce. Let's talk later," I said.

"I'm worried, Nia."

Her voice was low, just a hint above a whisper. I knew that when she spoke like that, she was troubled.

"I'll talk to you soon. Everything is *fine*, ma." I hung up the phone and studied Joyce. "Am I crazy?"

"A little bit, yeah." She chuckled, before she settled into a small smile and shrugged. "But I'm so excited for you. I think you've finally found your calling. It would be one thing if you were chasing a passion, but you're chasing purpose. That's God's will."

"I agree. I used to say that I was pursuing truth – chasing it, seeking it. I don't think I am anymore. I think it's finally found me," I said.

Joyce smiled and put her hand over mine before she nodded. "You can absolutely stay with me when your lease is over. We'll work something out." I held her hand and allowed mine to tremble in hers. I was terrified of leaping – terrified of what lied on the other side of my fear. But I was more afraid of never knowing, of standing still.

That evening, my voice shook with conviction as my mother and I entered hour two of our quarrel on the phone.

"You started a dance studio when I was three-months old. I think I deserve some empathy. You of all people know what it's like to dream," I said to her.

My mother hesitated on the other end of the phone. "I've held my tongue a lot since you graduated from Monroe, even when I didn't agree with your choices. I figured you didn't need my judgment, but now I'm not sure I know what you need from me."

"I need your support!"

She let a sigh escape before I heard some ice cubes clink around in her glass. "I told you before that dreams shape shift – that they're amorphous and I believe that. I suppose I should've also told you that dreaming is a privilege for many."

"I've got faith," I said softly. "I'm privileged too."

***

I stood in front of my bathroom mirror. The ends of my hair had grown ragged. My last cut grew back in a weird shape and it was dry after a few weeks of neglect. I walked down the street to a natural hair salon I'd passed everyday since I moved to Florida Avenue and I asked to be seen.

I sat on the edge of the styling chair and studied my dry hair in the mirror. I hadn't deep conditioned in months. My desiccated strands hadn't responded to coconut oil, heavy curl creams or hot oil treatments for a few weeks. The beautician pushed the hair apart and examined my scalp before she smiled at me. "This is salvageable. We just need to do a major trim and hydration treatment."

I studied the wild bush I'd tended to for years before I shook my head. "Cut it off."

She raised her eyebrows, before she pulled the hair down, revealing it was past my bra strap. "Cut it? I can get your hair to bounce back. Just give me an hour."

"Cut it. I want to start over."

She stared at me in the mirror. "Sweetheart, if this is because of a breakup or a rough season in your life, you'll get through this."

I laughed and shook my head. "I'm fine. I just want to start over. I brought some ideas for the cut."

I showed her the tapered cuts I wanted and she shook her head and mumbled under her breath while she cut the hair. It fell to the floor without struggle, and the shorter it got, the lighter I felt. I studied the new cut, tapered around the sides and in the back with more length on the top. I smiled a smile too big for my face. "I love this."

She managed to smile too before she nodded. "Looks cute on you. Fits your face."

Fits *me*, I thought.

Grant's back was turned when I met him for frozen yogurt that night. I called his name and he nodded, pulling down another lever. "I'm starting with this coconut tonight. What you thinking about?"

I grabbed a cup and stood next to him. He glanced over at me briefly before he froze. He looked at me once more, to confirm what he thought he'd seen. I studied his reaction – he was slow to respond. Finally, without warning, he wrapped his arms around me and kissed my cheek. "It's so good to see you."

"It's good to be seen."

Woman with a T.W.A.,
Woman with clipped stems,
Moisturize.
Flower.

EPILOGUE.

The sun extended its reach across the coffee shop and drenched empty tables with light. The busyness of the day subsided, ushering in the quiet evening. The smell of coffee beans remained. The silence swelled but it wasn't suffocating. Josie stopped the recorder and I exhaled a deep, slow, easy breath. This wasn't as hard as I thought it would be.

Josie and I cleared our table of the empty cups of tea we'd accumulated. She sat down and studied me as I grabbed a napkin. With my back to her, I dabbed at the corners of my eyes and put on a smile. I walked back to the table, grabbed my purse from the back of my chair and slid it on my shoulder. "Did you get what you needed?" I asked.

"A lot more," she said. She rested her chin in the palm of her hand. "You have an incredible story, Nia."

"Incredible," I repeated. I tried the word on for size. It felt much too big to describe me. "You hair is beautiful by the way. I meant to tell you."

"Thank you," Josie said.

I kept my hair short now. The longer it got, the more difficult it was for me to maintain it. As much as I appreciated the beauty of growth, the tangles and breakage were deterrents. It was simpler this way.

"Thank you for your honesty. Thank you for your willingness to open up. I'm really inspired by you and your journey," Josie said.

I didn't know how to internalize any of this. I didn't feel inspiring, especially these days. When I caught a glimpse of the time on my watch, I looked down at Josie. "I should get going. Grant is picking up dinner."

Josie stood up and smoothed out her dress before she stuck out her hand. I smiled and pulled her into a hug. "Good luck Josie."

"Thank you Nia," she said.

I scurried to the door. Josie looked at the date on her laptop before she called out to me. I stopped and turned to her.

"Happy birthday," she said softly.

It was my thirtieth birthday. I smiled and nodded before I walked out of the coffee shop and pulled out my phone. I had a few alerts from my fertility app and a missed call from Grant. We were trying to conceive. We'd been trying for sixteen months and I was growing more anxious with time. But Grant was incredibly patient like he'd always been. With my lupus under control, I was the healthiest I'd been in a long time. We were staying optimistic. We'd already painted our second bedroom in anticipation of it becoming a nursery.

"Your food is getting cold," he said when he answered the phone.

I didn't want to celebrate my birthday this year and Grant respected my wishes. He'd ordered takeout and I requested that we eat it on the floor of the living room, like old times.

"Well it sounds like you've already started eating," I said while I stood on the curb and ordered an Uber. A small smile lifted my lips.

Grant chewed his food and I could hear the TV on. I looked down at my wedding band and marveled at it. "Can't wait to see you."

"Same," he said. "See you soon."

Josie watched me from the coffee shop before she ordered a shot of espresso and opened her laptop. She was in for a long night. She created a new document and allowed the cursor to blink for a while before she began.

NIA LANDREY-CARTER:
THE STORIES WE TELL
Josephine Lawrence

Acknowledgement:

Thank you to Nia Landrey-Carter for your willingness to share your life with me. I hope that my words capture the fullness of your journey.

ABOUT THE AUTHOR

ELLE JEFFRIES is a native of Cleveland Heights, Ohio. She's a graduate of The Ohio State University and University of Maryland College Park. After writing under a pseudonym for a number of years, Elle decided to write in the light, with *Deep Condition* as her debut novel. She currently resides in Silver Spring, Maryland.